Cry for

the Moon

Cry for the Moon

Book One
The Last Werewolf Hunter

by

William Woodall

Jeremiah Press · *Antoine, Arkansas*

Jeremiah Press
PO Box 3
Antoine, AR 71922

Cover image by Julie King (jewelskings.deviantart.com), using model stock provided by auroradreams.deviantart.com. Used by permission.

First published by Jeremiah Press on 02/11/2009

Printed in the United States of America.

This book is printed on acid-free paper.

ISBN 978-0-9819641-1-9

Library of Congress Control Number: 2009920152

For Mathew,

For reminding me to be silly,
And also to be brave.

Love you, baby boy.

When my mother and father forsake me,
Then the Lord will take me up.
- Psalm 27:10

Thoughts of a Werewolf Hunter

"God is love, even to the lost, and to know Him at all is to know this."

"I couldn't go inside the store soaking wet and with no shoes on, unfortunately. They kinda frown on that, even in Arkansas."

"Duct tape glue is really nasty, just in case you ever wondered. I wouldn't advise chewing on it unless you absolutely have to. It gets stuck in between your teeth and I think they must flavor it with dirty motor oil, the way it tastes. I felt like gagging."

"Some people talk like making choices is easy as long as you know what you want, but that's just something stupid people say. I know better."

"Mama and Daddy didn't really care how I felt or what I thought about things. It was almost like any other boy in the world would have done just as well to fill my place. That bites, you know."

"As long as I live, when I think about Louisiana, I'll remember glistening mist on a Cajun girl's hair, and walking together under those live oak trees, and being happy."

"There are only three questions a man ever needs to ask: What is the nature of God, what things are worth living for, and what things are worth dying for. And the answer to all of them is the same: only love."

"The only reason we ever love anybody or anything in the world is because they remind us of God in some way, like the reflection of the sun in a dew drop. I believe that with my whole heart, and when Jolie told me about the Hope of the werewolf hunters, how could I keep from loving her for that?"

"You can never have the same thing twice, and it's hopeless to try. It never works like that, and all you end up doing is breaking your heart against a solid rock. That's why when you lose things you have to let them go instead of trying to get them back again. You can't do it, and you only hurt yourself worse if you keep on. Never cry for the moon."

"Sometimes you have to just be, to take time to praise God in silence like the rocks and the trees and the clouds in the sky do, so that you get closer to Him and see with His eyes. If you spend your whole life running hard, then you never have time to grow."

Contents

Chapter One

I didn't know anything special was going on when Nana Maralyn asked me to go walking with her in the apple orchard that day.

It was late one evening after supper was over, and we walked on tiptoes so we could listen to the crickets. Nana always used to tell me they were like people, and sang their prettiest songs whenever they were saddest, when they knew that winter was coming. She used to say stuff like that all the time. It was late October in Tennessee, so I guess they didn't have much time left.

Nana kept quiet, but I could feel the soft crease in her palm where she rested her hand on my bare shoulder. Her claws were really sharp that night, digging into my skin like tacks, and I shifted my weight uncomfortably.

"Be still, Zach," she commanded. I quit squirming; Nana had a way of pinching the very blood out of you when you didn't mind her.

I was only twelve then, and I remember I went barefooted, knowing it might be for the last time that year. I liked the feel of the grass tickling between my toes, and felt sorry for Nana Maralyn in her big black boots.

By and by we came to the little clearing with the big flat rock sticking up out of the ground. Nana smiled, and went ahead of me so she could go sit on the rock. She closed her eyes at first and took a deep breath, then opened them and looked at me.

"Come here, Zach," she said, holding out her arms to me. I went to her and sat down, wondering what she wanted. She took a little flute from her purse and began to play a song I thought I might have heard before, but I wasn't sure. It made me sleepy, and when Nana Maralyn got up and nudged me down flat on my back on the rock, I didn't resist her very much. I could hardly keep my eyes open.

She went on playing that tune for a long time, and I wasn't exactly sure when it finished. I think I might have gone to sleep, because the next thing I remember was Nana painting something cool and wet on my chest. It felt kind of nice, but when she tried to put something in my mouth I opened my eyes to see what she was doing.

Moonlight flooded down all around us from the fat full moon. Nana had the sparkly perfume bottle in her hand, and held my mouth open while she shook a few drops of blood on my tongue.

"Oh, yuck, Nana, you know I hate blood," I murmured feebly, trying to spit and sputter. Nana wouldn't let me, and finally I swallowed it just to get rid of the nasty taste. She started playing her flute again after that and I drifted back to sleep.

The next time I woke up it was morning, and I was still lying cold and stiff on that darned rock. Nana Maralyn was nowhere to be seen. I couldn't believe she'd left me to sleep outside all night.

I sat up and looked at my bare chest, which was covered with symbols painted on with some kind of gritty white paint. It flaked off when I touched it and smelled like old cough drops or Mentholatum. I scraped it off me and stood up, shivering a little. I knew what had happened, then. Nana Maralyn had done the Ceremony on me.

I was suddenly furious at her for tricking me like that, and I walked back to the house fuming.

They were all waiting for me, of course, happy and pleased as punch. They always were, the morning after going hunting under a full moon, but today they seemed extra specially jolly. Mama had baked a cake like it was my birthday or something, and Nana Maralyn smiled and kissed me. Daddy picked me up with a huge bear-hug and said, "My boy's all grown up today!" like it was the proudest day of his life. Even my little sister Lola was grinning at me with that gap-toothed grille of hers.

I'd been getting into a blacker mood with every passing second, and finally I couldn't hold back any longer.

"I don't want to be a monster!" I screamed, about to cry and even more furious at them because of that.

The smile faded from Nana Maralyn's lips, and Daddy looked like somebody had suddenly stuck a lemon in his mouth. There was dead silence in the kitchen.

"Yes, well, I guess we all felt that way at first, Zach," Daddy finally said, with a forced laugh. He clearly had never felt that way, but his comment broke the ice and let everybody go back to joking and bustling around. He put me down and I stalked off to the corner, pretending I was headed for the cookie jar back there, but really I just wanted to be left alone. I was still madder than a long tailed cat in a room full of rocking chairs. But of course I couldn't get away that easily.

"Once you get used to it I know you'll change your mind, Zach. It's not nice to be so nasty and make everybody unhappy, is it?" Mama whispered to me. I couldn't help feeling guilty when she put it like that, so I tried to smile and let on like I was convinced. I wasn't happy though, and I think they could tell. I slipped away as soon as I could and went up to my room.

It was Saturday, but since there was nothing else to do I tried to work on my math homework. It was easy stuff, so that didn't last too long. I cupped my chin in my hands and wondered how long it would be before my claws would start growing, and what rabbit guts really tasted like. Would I like them better with salt, or ketchup, or maybe cheese? I laughed, even though it wasn't really all that funny. I pushed my tongue around my canine teeth, imagining that they already felt sharper.

Maybe I ought to explain a few things. Everybody in my family except me and Lola is a monster. They get mad at me when I use that word, but it's the truth, isn't it? Daddy says the right name for what we are is *loup-garou*, but I don't care; as far as I'm concerned a monster is a monster. Lola's not old enough to be one yet, cause she's only six. It's not that you have to be any certain age; it's just that they couldn't trust her to behave herself.

But anyway, whenever they decide she's old enough, they'll take her out to a flat rock somewhere, and put her to sleep, and paint the right symbols on her chest with peppermint and henbane, and put a little blood in her mouth, and leave her to sleep all night under the Hunter's Moon. I never used to know that every full moon in the year has its own special name, but they do, and none of the others will work except that one. I don't know why, but that's what Nana Maralyn told me.

I had known for a long time that I would probably have to be a monster when I grew up. I was never very happy about it, and they all knew how I felt. I'm not sure why I hated the idea so much. I just never could get excited over the thought of killing something and tearing it to pieces with my bare hands just for the fun of it; not even a rabbit or a deer. It didn't seem right, somehow, and the older I got the less I liked it.

They always used to tell me I'd grow out of feeling that way. I never did, though, and the fact that all of them had gotten in cahoots together to trick me into it anyway, whether I liked it or not. . . I was pretty steamed, let me tell you. That was the last straw, as far as I was concerned. They could go out and eat rabbits and toads and rats all day long if they felt like it, but I wasn't having any part of it.

If I could only think how.

Almost a month went by and I never felt any different, so I started to get curious. I wolfed down my lunch at school and spent every second I could spare in the library, reading books about monsters and werewolves and things like that. The other kids started to notice it after a while, but I said I was doing a special report for the young authors' fair. That got me off the hook; everybody knows how much I like to write.

Most of the books were stupid, but I finally hit paydirt with a book about monsters that mentioned *loup-garous* on one page, even though it only had a little blurb about them that didn't tell me much. It said they were produced by a special kind of curse on ordinary people, and that silver was poisonous to a *loup-garou*, but only if they got scratched with it or it got in their blood some kind of way. I didn't see how that part could really help me much, though. I didn't want to fight one, I just wanted to keep from having to become one myself.

On the other hand, the idea that you had to be cursed before you could become a *loup-garou* gave me an awful lot to think about. Nobody ever told me about that part of it before. I knew what a curse was, and when I found out that's what was really happening it kinda scared me, to tell the truth. It made me wonder what all else I didn't know.

So then I started looking up stuff about curses and ways to cure them. They only mentioned one cure in the *loup-garou* book, and I didn't like it. It said that you had to take the cursed person and strip him naked, and then have twelve girls beat him with switches from an alder tree by the light of a full moon until he fainted. I decided to pass that one up unless I absolutely had no other choice. I wasn't sure what alder was, anyway, and how would I ever live such a thing down? I'd never be able to show my face at school again for the rest of my life.

I got my act together at home, too. I convinced everybody that I was thrilled about becoming a *loup-garou*, and I got them to tell me stories and answer questions. Daddy seemed especially pleased with all this interest, so he was the one I worked on the hardest. Oh, I laid it on thick.

Me and my dad had never really talked much or been close, but this was something he cared about. We had several long discussions, and one day I mentioned, like it didn't interest me much, that I'd read somewhere that it was possible to "cure" a *loup-garou* and turn him back into a regular person. He looked instantly suspicious for a minute.

"What have you been reading, Zach?" he demanded, scowling.

"It was only a story," I said smoothly, and told him about the ceremony with the switches and the twelve girls. He laughed until his face turned red and tears squeezed from the corners of his eyes.

"I'd give my eyeteeth to see it, Zach, but I'm afraid when it was over you'd simply have a very sore young *loup-garou* the next day," he said. I tried to show how relieved I was to hear that, and I think it must have encouraged him to trust me.

"No, Zach, you don't have to worry about anybody trying to cure you. It can't be done. The only way to cure a *loup-garou* is not to ever become one at all. After next week you've got nothing to worry about," he promised me.

I pounced on that.

"Really? What's next week?" I asked innocently, already plotting how I might avoid it.

"Well, next week's the full moon again, and of course you can't really be a full-fledged *loup-garou* until you make your first kill that night," he said.

That was a very interesting little tidbit of information, and I filed it away for more thought later. In the meantime, I put on my best worried look.

"But what if I'm sick that night or something?" I asked anxiously. Daddy thought about that awhile.

"Hmm, well, now, that's a good question, Zach. I can't remember a time when it ever happened before, but if it did then I guess it would mean you'd have to wait another year and redo everything next October," he said. He paused a few seconds, and looked at me with his brow wrinkled up, like he was trying to guess what I was thinking.

"I wouldn't worry about it though; I'm sure everything will be fine," he finally said. He smiled a toothy grin because he knew it would make me laugh, and that was all we said about it.

I laid in bed that night with my eyes open for a long time, just thinking about stuff. I had my answer now about how to keep from becoming a monster (or *loup-garou*, or werewolf, or whatever the heck you wanted to call it), but the problem was, I didn't like the answer much. I would have rather just stripped naked and let the girls beat me with switches than what I was going to have to do instead. That would have been over in one night, but this was forever. I was going to have to run away.

Oh, I know what you're thinking. It was a crazy idea, and surely there must have been an easier way if I'd only thought about it awhile longer. But see, I didn't have the time to think very long, and I knew my family real well. This was a really big deal to them.

I could maybe do something to botch up this year's hunt and make them have to wait and curse me again next fall, but even that wasn't a sure thing. Even if I pretended to be deathly sick, they could probably still bring a mouse in my room and make me kill it, and after that it would all be over. But suppose I did manage to mess it up? What then?

They'd be suspicious then, that's what. They'd keep me locked up in the attic all year if they had to, and then I really wouldn't have any way to escape. There wouldn't be any room to talk about it and they wouldn't take no for an answer, ever. They were so convinced that being a monster was the best thing since sliced bread, it was hopeless to try to change their minds. If I wanted to stay myself and not be cursed, then the only choice I had was to leave. It was that simple. I knew that just as sure as God made little green apples.

Knowing all that, it didn't take much thought before I decided I had to get away now, while they still thought I loved the idea of being a monster.

The really hard part was, I knew I could never come back. Some people talk like making choices is easy as long as you know what you want, but that's just something stupid people say. I know better.

I looked over at my window, where the moon was pouring in through the curtains, bright and big and almost full. There wasn't much time left.

Chapter Two

I slipped out of bed like a cat, not making the least bit of noise. Nana especially had very good ears, and she wasn't far down the hall. I didn't turn on the light or anything because I didn't want to attract attention, and the moon was bright enough to see by anyway.

Once I made up my mind, there were some things I needed to do right away to get ready. I wasn't sure exactly when the next full moon would be, but it couldn't be more than three or four days off at the most. Tomorrow was Friday, and I was afraid it might come before I had another school day. Daddy had said "next week", but that could mean Sunday for all I knew. My best bet was to get away while everybody thought I was at school, because then I'd have almost a whole day before anybody thought to look for me. That meant I needed to leave tomorrow, because Monday might be too late.

I tiptoed across the room and got my backpack from the floor beside my desk. Then I very quietly and carefully emptied all the books out, making sure to slide them 'way far on the top shelf of the closet where maybe nobody would see them or think to look. I kept *Robinson Crusoe* with me though, so I'd have something to read. I bought it at the book fair at school a week ago and I was only about halfway finished with it.

For clothes, I gathered some jeans and t-shirts and other things and put them in the bottom of the backpack, making sure to roll them up as tight as I could so they wouldn't take up as much room. I didn't dare take *all* my clothes, you know; somebody might notice that. So I just took an extra pair of everything. That way I could wear one set while I washed the other.

I took my Swiss Army knife too, just in case. Whenever Robinson Crusoe got in a pickle, he always had to have tools and weapons and things, so I figured I'd better have something too. You never knew what you might run into. I didn't think I'd get captured by cannibals or anything, but if I did then I wanted to be ready.

I also took my little radio and headphones that I got for Christmas last year, just for something to do. I couldn't use it too much because it ate batteries like candy, but I thought it would be good to have it just in case.

Money would have helped a lot, but all I had was twenty-four dollars and ten cents. I'd been saving it up in a sock stuffed back behind everything in the top drawer of my desk, but I knew it wasn't much. Mama and Daddy were too stingy to give me an allowance or anything, so I had to pick up cash whenever I got the chance, running errands and stuff like that.

If it had been just two weeks ago I would have had almost a hundred bucks from raking yards and stuff, but I spent most of that at the book fair. I wished I had it back, now. But Mama always said there's no use crying over spilt milk, so I'd just have to make what I had last for as long as I could. Maybe I could rake some more leaves or mow grass or something like that if I had to.

There was also food to think about, and that was a tough one. There wasn't much I could carry with me because it was so darned bulky. I didn't mind drinking water all the time, but food was different. I knew a little bit about what you could eat and what was poisonous out in the woods, but I couldn't live on acorn soup and dandelion salad all the time. I could catch fish, maybe, but that would get awfully old after awhile.

I was smart enough to know there might come a point when I'd be glad to have a fish, no matter how tired I was of them, so I took a box of hooks and a roll of fishing line from my tackle box and stuffed them in the backpack with my clothes. You don't really need anything else in a pinch, cause you can always dig up worms and cut a cane pole most anywhere. You don't even have to have a bobber, but if I wanted one I could use a little piece of dry wood.

That was about all I had in my own room that was worth taking, but there were still some other things I needed from the rest of the house.

For one thing, I needed some way to light a fire. I knew there was a box of lighters downstairs in the drawer next to the refrigerator, and I decided to take all of those. Lighting fires is a lot easier that way than if you try to do all that stuff with sparks and dry wood shavings. They taught us how to do that at Cub Scouts, and I thought it was silly even back then. I might be a country boy, but I wasn't an idiot.

I slipped downstairs quiet as a mouse and got myself a glass of chocolate milk from the refrigerator. That way if anybody heard me and came to see what I was doing, I had a good excuse for being up.

I rummaged around in the drawer until I found the lighters. There were three of them left, and I stuck them in my pocket. I found some extra double-A batteries for my radio in there and I took those too. Then I collected all the food I thought I could carry that wouldn't be missed and wouldn't spoil. There was beef jerky, candy bars, some string cheese, a couple of little cans of Beanie Weenies, and three apples. That should get me by for a little while at least.

I was pretty satisfied that I had all the basics covered at that point.

You might be thinking I forgot about the main thing in all this, like where I meant to go after I left. You'd be wrong though. I knew I was in a tight spot and didn't have too many choices right then, and that's really what scared me the most. It would be worse than doing nothing at all if I ran away and then got caught in a day or two, cause I knew I'd never get a second chance. Let alone how embarrassing it would be.

My friend Jonathan ran away last year, for a little while. He ended up back home the very next day, as soon as he got hungry. I didn't think I'd have *that* to worry about, anyway, but the problem of where to go was a tough nut to crack.

My first idea was to go out into the wild country behind the house and hide out for a couple of weeks until people stopped looking for me so hard. I could camp out in the woods for that long, if I had to, and while I was there I could think about what to do next. But the more I thought about it, the less I liked that idea. People went in there to go hiking and fishing and stuff all the time, and even worse than that, Daddy and Mama and Nana hunted there whenever there was a full moon. I was willing to bet my beard they'd look around out there first before they did anything else.

Oh, I don't really have a beard, you know. But Mama always said I shouldn't gamble and so I couldn't bet something real, could I? Anyway, I didn't dare go somewhere like that, even for a little while. It was too risky.

So what other choices did I have?

Well, I could have asked one of my friends to hide me out for a while. Jonathan probably would, if I asked him. Or if he couldn't, then there were a couple of others. The only problem with that was, I wasn't sure I trusted any of them not to spill the beans and get me caught sooner or later. Probably sooner.

No, definitely not, come to think of it. A secret like that was just too juicy not to tell somebody, and then that person has to tell somebody else, and then before you know it everybody knows. And even if they *could* keep their mouth shut, I knew they couldn't hide me out forever. It would only be putting off the problem, not solving it.

I sat there racking my brain trying to come up with a solution till I thought I might start to see smoke coming out of my ears. I started to wonder if there even *was* a solution.

Then I hit on a good one, I thought; my uncle Justin. I'm not sure what made me think of him right then. I'd never met him, and I wasn't sure if he even knew I existed. Nobody had talked to him since before I was even born, as far as I knew.

All I knew about him was a picture I'd seen in the back of Mama's photo album. He was her younger brother and (I gathered) not a monster. I was never really clear on why not; Mama wouldn't say much about him. I just knew he wasn't one and that because of that nobody would have anything to do with him.

The only other thing I knew was that he lived somewhere in Texas, or at least he did the last time anybody heard anything. That's where Mama and Daddy were both from, so there was a good chance Justin might still live there.

I knew Daddy grew up on Stonewall Street in Sulphur Springs, because I remembered hearing him and Nana mention it before. I wasn't totally sure about Mama, but I figured she couldn't have lived too awful far from there.

She wasn't a monster till she met Daddy while they were in college, but then they moved to Tennessee and that was that. I guess there were more rabbits there or something. . . I really don't know.

I'd never thought much about Justin before, but now I started to wonder if he might help me. He was the only family I had who wasn't a monster, and surely that meant something, didn't it? Of course he didn't know me from Adam and who could tell what he might think if I just showed up on his doorstep. I didn't know what kind of man he was, if he was rich or poor, nasty or kind, or anything at all really. I might never even find him. If you think finding a man named Justin Wilder who (maybe) lives somewhere in Texas is an easy thing to do, just try it sometime.

The only thing I had to go on for sure was that picture in Mama's album, and it must have been at least ten years old. Could I even still recognize him after all that time? Could anybody? In the picture he was about sixteen, a thin and wiry sort of guy with a blond goatee and a smile that reminded me a little bit of the way Mama smiled sometimes.

I quit thinking about how hopeless it was, so it wouldn't get me down. I'm not sure exactly when I decided for sure I'd try to find Justin, but the more I thought about it the less I could think of any better idea.

I wasn't even really sure how to go about it, except to head for Sulphur Springs and see what I found when I got there. I know it sounds like a hare-brained scheme, but like I said I really didn't have much time to think. I had to get out of town before I lost my only chance. I figured I could decide what to do next after I got to Texas.

But if that was the plan, then I needed one more thing. I catfooted into the living room and pulled Mama's picture album off the bookshelf. I took the whole thing, partly because I didn't want them to guess where I was going (which they might do if only the picture of Justin was missing), but mostly because there were pictures of everyone else in there too, and I didn't want to forget them.

I didn't think anybody would notice the album was missing. Mama digitized all her photos a long time ago and stores them on CD now, mostly; she likes computers. If anybody did notice the album was gone, it was a thousand to one they'd ever connect it with me. And even if they did, they wouldn't guess why.

I slipped back upstairs and put the food and the batteries and the picture album in my backpack along with the other stuff, then I zipped it up tight and went back to bed.

In the morning I acted like it was a normal day. I got ready for school just like always and ate a couple of extra pancakes for breakfast. I surprised Mama by giving her a kiss before I left. I hadn't done that in a while, and I didn't know if I'd ever have the chance again.

"What was that for?" she asked me, laughing a little and putting her hand up to her cheek.

"Just because," I told her, with an innocent look. She smiled again and smoothed my hair down a bit, like she did every morning, and then she sent me down to the end of the lane to wait for the school bus. She usually took Lola to school herself a little later on, and with a little luck nobody would know I was missing until sometime late this afternoon.

When I didn't come home after school, they'd probably start calling around to see where I was, and then it wouldn't take long for them to find out I hadn't been at school that day. That's when things would start to get hairy, and I knew I'd better be long gone before then. I figured I had about eight hours to make my getaway, maybe nine if I was really lucky.

I slipped into the edge of the woods on the far side of the highway, making sure I was far enough into the trees that nobody could possibly see me from the road. Before long the bus came along and stopped at our lane, just in case I was a little late getting out this morning. Then when I didn't come out, it went on again. You couldn't see the highway from the house, so I didn't have to worry about anybody noticing that I didn't get on the bus.

I waited till it was completely out of sight before I came out of the woods again. I had maybe thirty minutes before Mama came by with Lola, and during that time I had to do something quick.

I headed south along the highway, since that was the direction I needed to be going anyway. It was a good thing Mama would be going the other way with Lola, but I knew I couldn't count on that to last. She might decide to visit one of her friends that lived down this way or go grocery shopping or something like that.

I should have taken my bike, but I didn't dare go back home for it now. Nana Maralyn would be at home all day and she would be full of questions about why I wasn't at school. So I walked.

There weren't any houses close to ours. I'm not sure if my mom and dad planned it that way or not, but it meant there wasn't anybody much to see me walking down the highway. Of course, it also meant there wasn't much traffic and nobody who might give me a ride. I walked almost till noon before I came to the edge of town, and I knew that wouldn't do. I had to make better time than that.

I was beginning to worry that I wouldn't be able to get far enough away from home by the end of the day to keep them from finding me. It wasn't looking good, unless I found a way to get somewhere that was faster than my own two feet.

I thought about getting a bus ticket, but I wasn't sure if I had enough money for that, and besides, I was afraid the girl at the ticket counter would remember me later if people asked. If she did, she might tell them where I went and get me caught as soon as I stepped off the bus.

What I really needed was to get as far away as I could, as quick as I could, with nobody noticing. That was shaping up to be harder than I thought.

There's a big truck stop close to the interstate in our town, and I finally decided I'd go down there and see if I could scrounge a ride somewhere. I really didn't even care where it was at that point, as long as it was far away from home. I could figure out how to get to Texas later, when the wolves weren't so hot on my heels.

I got to the truck stop about two o'clock, I guess. I knew my time was running out, so I started nosing around the parked trucks. The best thing would be if I could stow away in one of them, because then even the driver wouldn't know I was there, but that's not as easy as it sounds. Most of the trucks are locked up tight until they get to wherever they're going, so you can't get inside. But if you're smart and if you have just a smidgen of luck, you can still find ways.

I had to be careful out in that parking lot. Drivers don't like it when they see people hanging around their trucks. They always think you're trying to steal something or slash their tires or just that you're generally up to no good. I didn't want that. So I pretended I was looking for pocket change. You can almost always find some in a big parking lot, if you look for awhile. If somebody saw me staring at the pavement instead of the trucks, they might just possibly not bother.

I finally found a flat-bed truck that was carrying a load of septic tanks, and that suited me just fine. I could open up one of the tanks and crawl down inside where nobody would ever think to look for me, and there was plenty of room in one of them. Go ahead and laugh at me if you want to; I bet you couldn't have found anything better in such a tight spot.

I glanced around to make sure nobody was looking. The flatbed was screened off from the store and the gas pumps by two other tall trucks parked on each side of it, so I was ninety-nine percent sure nobody could see me.

I grabbed the edge of the bed and hoisted myself up, using one of the tires for a stepping stone. The tanks were sitting upright on the bed, tied down with steel hawsers to keep them from falling over. I wasn't sure I'd be able to climb up one of them until I found a way of scrunching myself in between two tanks and working my way up like I was climbing a tree. They were made of concrete, so that helped a lot because of the friction. Plastic ones would have been much harder to deal with.

Anyway, I finally got to the top of the first one in line and unfastened the lid. It was just clear plastic, so I popped it off without too much trouble and eeled my way down inside the tank. It was dark in there at first until my eyes adjusted.

The tank was about three feet across and maybe six feet high. Not big enough to be really comfortable, but not as bad as it could have been. I was able to reach up and pull myself out when I needed to, and that was important. I didn't even want to imagine how embarrassing it would be to get stuck inside a sewage tank and be discovered there whenever the truck got to wherever it was going.

I fixed the lid back in place so nobody would have any reason to come looking at the tank I was in. Then I sat down on the concrete floor and rested my back against the wall. It curved out just a little bit, so that made it pretty comfortable.

Then I waited.

And waited, and waited some more. I started to think that dude would never leave. Even the extra large all-you-can-eat catfish plate and a really hot shower doesn't take that long to finish.

It must have been almost two hours before I finally heard somebody messing around making sure the tie-down lines were tight, and then I knew we'd be on our way soon. A good thing too, because I should have been home thirty minutes ago. It wouldn't be long before the hunt was up, if it wasn't already.

I heard the door of the truck slam and felt the vibration when the engine started up, and finally we started to move.

I felt the truck bounce through a pothole as it pulled out onto the highway, rattling my tank and making me hit my head against the wall. The driver stopped again after a minute, I guessed at the red light. Not long after that I felt us get on the interstate, but I couldn't have told you which way he was headed to save my life. It does funny things to your sense of direction when you can't see where you're going. The truck settled down to a steady speed, and that was that.

I let out a sigh of relief. The odds were a thousand to one that anybody would ever find me now.

Chapter Three

Like I said, I had no idea which way we were headed. I knew the interstate ran east-west through our town, but that didn't help me much. The truck might be bound for almost anywhere. All I could do was hope it took me somewhere far from home but not too far from Texas.

I was afraid to poke my head up out of the lid and see the signs, because either the lid might blow away in the wind or else the driver (or somebody else) might see me and tell somebody. So I had to be content with not knowing for a while. I figured I'd find out soon enough, if I was patient.

It gets darned boring, just sitting around for hours inside a concrete tank with nothing to do and nobody to talk to. If you don't believe me, try it sometime. There was nothing to see and not even anything to hear except the muffled traffic noises. I didn't want to use the radio batteries unless I absolutely had to. I didn't know when I might need them.

Enough light filtered down through the lid for me to read if I wanted to, so I laid down on the floor of the tank and stuffed my backpack behind my head for a pillow and read

Robinson Crusoe for awhile till it started to get dark outside. It wasn't real cold, not yet anyway. The concrete held in my body heat and kept it pretty warm inside.

I started to get hungry, so I ate an apple and a can of Beanie Weenies and some string cheese. I used the spoon on my Swiss Army knife to eat the beans, telling myself the whole time how smart I was that I remembered to bring it along. It would have been nice to have something to drink, but I survived without it.

After that, since I couldn't read anymore, I gave in and turned on the radio for awhile. I thought maybe I'd hear one of the dj's mention where his station was, and then maybe I'd know which way the truck was going.

After awhile I heard a station in Memphis, so I knew I was headed west. At least for now I was. That was a big relief, even though I knew the truck might turn some other way at any time.

I was getting drowsy by then, so I turned off the radio and tried to sleep.

It got darned cold inside that tank before morning came, let me tell you. I woke up shivering my toes off a long time before the sun came up. It was so cold I could see my breath in the air, even in the weak light.

I pulled out my extra clothes and tried to cover up with them the best I could, but it didn't do much good. I laid there miserable and freezing for the rest of the night, sometimes dozing a little bit but mostly not. I think that was one of the most horrible nights I ever spent in my whole entire life.

The driver ended up dropping his load sometime early the next morning. It was still dark when I noticed him get off the interstate. He did some stop and start driving through town for a while, and then he parked the truck. I heard him disconnecting the trailer and felt the jerk when he pulled loose from it. The sound of the truck gradually moved away, and then everything was quiet again. Nobody had ever noticed I was there.

I waited just a little while, until I was sure the truck was out of sight, and then I stood up. I felt colder than a pair of brass underwear. I stuffed all my gear back inside my backpack, and then popped the lid off the tank with my fist and poked my head out to see what kind of place I was in.

The trailer was parked next to a bunch of others in a big lot by a warehouse. Or something like that; I couldn't tell for sure what it was from the outside. It was just a huge gray building that looked like it was big enough to hold a football stadium. I didn't see any people or machines moving around.

It was a frosty morning, with just a little bit of ice around the rim of some mud puddles on the parking lot. The sun was just barely up, and it was real quiet and still, like it usually is at that time of day. I shivered again and put on the other t-shirt from my backpack on top of the one I was already wearing. It wasn't enough to keep out all the cold, but it helped a lot. I wished I'd brought a jacket. You always end up needing the stuff you forgot at the worst possible times, don't you?

I let the tank lid slide down and hit the dirt, then scrambled out onto the flatbed. I jumped the last few feet to the ground, being careful not to twist an ankle. The parking lot was deserted, but I knew that probably wouldn't last. People would be coming to work sooner or later and I needed to be well gone by then. It was Saturday, but that was no guarantee the place would be closed.

There was a tall chain link fence around the property, with no gate that I could see. I wouldn't have minded climbing over it, except it was topped with barbed wire and that stuff hurts. I guess it was supposed to keep people out, but it did a real good job of keeping me inside too.

So I explored a little bit. That parking lot must have been big enough to land a plane in. It probably took me fifteen minutes to walk to the end of it, and I still couldn't find any gate. I'm sure it must have *had* one, of course. The truck that brought me there must have got in somewhere, but I was blessed if I could find it. The only break in the fence I found was where the corner post met the edge of the building, and that wasn't wide enough for me to squeeze through.

I was starting to worry. I could hear sounds now from the other side of the building, muffled booms and growls like somebody was running heavy equipment over there a long way off, and there was getting to be more traffic on the street. Somebody would find me inside the fence if I didn't hurry up and bust out of there.

I stood there for a minute not sure what to do, then I remembered my trusty Swiss Army knife. It had a little pair of wire cutters on it. I didn't know if they would be strong enough to cut chain link, but it might be worth a try.

I fished out my knife and opened it up. Those little cutters looked pitiful, I tell you. I didn't think they would work, but I shook my head and tried it anyway. I figured I didn't have anything to lose.

And you know, they did work, finally. I bet it took me five minutes to cut just one link in that fence, and my hand was hurting by the time it broke in two.

I threw my knife down in disgust and took a few steps to let the building block the wind from hitting me. There wasn't much of it, but even that little bit was too cold for comfort. I stood there breathing warm air on my hurt hand and sticking it under my arm pit to make it feel better. Finally it did.

Maybe I could have cut my way out with those clippers, if I'd had a week to work on it. But I didn't have that much time, so I needed to think of something else.

After awhile I got to looking at the fence a little closer, and I noticed there really wasn't anything holding those links together. They were just long strands of twisted metal braided together and stretched tight. I guess I always knew that, sort of, but I never paid attention before. I never *needed* to pay attention before.

I took hold of the cut end of the link I'd snipped in two and moved it back and forth to make sure. It definitely wasn't attached to anything. I pushed the tip of it down real hard and discovered that I could undo the weave of the fence if I was careful. It was sorta like braiding my sister's hair, or unbraiding it I guess, except her hair feels a little nicer than chain link.

It still hurt my fingers and it wasn't easy, and I still had to take the wire cutters to it one more time before I was done, but after about thirty minutes I opened up a hole I thought would be big enough for me to worm through.

I put my backpack outside first, then I stuck my head through the fence. So far so good. I had to push hard to get my shoulders through, but once that was done I thought I was home free.

Didn't turn out that way, naturally. I was squirming my way through and the dadgummed fence snagged on my belt buckle. I don't know how it happened, but I couldn't move either direction. I struggled and kicked and got scratched and sweaty in spite of the cold, and by the time I finally broke free I ended up ripping a big hole in the front of my pants right next to the zipper. That made me mad, so I turned around and kicked that fence as hard as I could.

Probably not the smartest thing I ever did, cause the fence didn't feel it, but you can bet your sweet cream I did. It hurt!

So there I was with a sweaty face and a sore foot and holey pants, looking like I just came out of a fight with a bobcat. I was glad nobody was around to see me like that.

I patched the fence up a little so maybe nobody would notice it had been cut, and then I started walking south along the street. Nobody yelled anything while I was walking away.

The sun was up by then, and it was beginning to get just a little bit warmer. That was good, because the hole in my pants was freezing me to death. I held my backpack in front of me, partly to block the wind and partly to keep from showing off my boxers to the whole wide world. Mama still thought it was *so* cute to get me Spiderman underwear, and there was no way I wanted anybody to see *that*.

After I got far enough down the road to be out of sight of the warehouse, I started noticing cross streets now and then. I looked at the street signs, and that's how I found out I was on Zero Street. I thought it was a strange name. It made me think of candy bars, but maybe that's just because I was hungry.

I sat down on the curb and rummaged in my backpack to see what I could find for breakfast. I've got to tell you, the pickings looked mighty thin. I ate some beef jerky and a piece of chocolate, and spent fifty cents at a Coke machine to get a Mello Yello. It wasn't a very good breakfast, I'm afraid. I sat there the whole time thinking about sausage and scrambled eggs.

There seemed to be a lot of industrial-type buildings around me; warehouses and factories and stuff like that, with a convenience store sprinkled in there now and then just to spice things up.

I walked into one of the stores, and the first thing I did was go in the bathroom and change my pants. I threw the old ones in the trash, because there was no way they could be fixed and I didn't see any reason to lug them around for nothing.

As soon as that was done, I went up to the counter and asked to see the phone book. It was fabulously, deliciously warm inside that store, and I was in no hurry to leave. I sat down at one of the booths by the front window and opened the book. That's how I found out I was in Fort Smith, Arkansas.

I wasn't sure where that was, but there was also a map in the front of the directory. I was on the western border of Arkansas, kinda up toward the north.

That was a pretty cool thing to know, and it encouraged me. I was a lot closer to Texas than when I started out. But on the other hand, it was still an awful long way off. Getting the rest of the way down there was the problem now.

I wasn't nearly in the rush I was when I was just trying to get as far from home as I could without getting caught, and I could afford to take some time to think about what I needed to do.

I didn't think it would be a good idea to try to hitch a ride on another truck, for the simple reason that I could never be sure which way it was headed or where I might end up. What if next time I wound up in California or Yukon or something? It might turn out to be awful hard to get back from some of those places. It just wasn't worth the risk. I was lucky to be as close as I was.

After a lot of thinking, I decided it might be worthwhile to buy a bus ticket this time. That way I could be sure where I was going and it wouldn't take that long for me to get there. Nobody knew me here, and they hopefully wouldn't have any reason to remember me unless I did something dumb.

I leafed my way through the phone book until I found the Greyhound station, then I went to one of the pay phones outside and called them.

The woman who answered the phone thought I was a girl at first and that aggravated me, but I kept my mouth shut and let her go ahead thinking so. I wanted information more than I wanted respect right then. She told me a ticket to Sulphur Springs would cost me about forty-five dollars, more or less.

That was bad news. I only had about half that much, and I wasn't sure how I could get the rest, unless maybe I raked leaves or something. I couldn't help noticing there were plenty of them to be raked.

I was fairly warm by then, so I gave the phone book back to the man at the counter and decided I better get started.

I hotfooted it down the street until I got to what seemed to be a residential type area with some nice houses. Most of them were already raked, but there are always a few places where people just don't have the energy or the time to get it done.

I went up to one of those places and knocked on the door. It had a big brass knocker in the shape of a lion's head, which was cool. I like unusual things like that.

At first nobody came to the door and I started to think maybe nobody was home. Finally I heard the door unlatch and creak open. There was a little old woman with blue hair standing in the doorway. She had on thick glasses with gold rims and didn't seem to know why I was there.

"Would you like your leaves raked today, ma'am?" I asked politely. She looked me over and seemed to think about it a minute, like she was trying to decide if I was a bloodthirsty criminal or not.

"I'll give you ten dollars," she finally said. That was highway robbery, but I had to smile and say "Sure!" I needed the money too much to haggle about it.

It took me three hours to rake that darned yard. It was a big one, and it turned out to be a breezy day. The leaves kept blowing back across the places I'd already cleared up, which made it take ten times as long as it should have. When I was finally done, hot and sweaty and tired, I collected my ten dollars and moved on.

The rest of the day I only found two other yards that needed raking, and they were little ones. They still paid me more than that stingy old skinflint with the blue hair, though. I got fifteen dollars for each yard, which meant I had about sixty-three bucks in my pocket by the end of the day. That ought to be enough to buy the bus ticket I needed, with a little bit left over.

Chapter Four

I was tired and dirty from raking leaves all day, and I didn't feel like walking to the Greyhound station. I took a city bus instead, which was something I'd never done before. I had to ask another kid at the bus stop how much it cost and how you could tell where the bus was going and all that good stuff. It's always embarrassing when you have to admit you don't know things everybody else takes for granted.

When I finally got to the bus station there was a long line of people waiting at the counter to buy tickets. Things were moving slower than granny's molasses, but since I had no choice I just stood there and waited my turn. After a while my mind started wandering, and I got to thinking about what I might do after I made it to Sulphur Springs.

The simplest thing would be to open a phone book and see if Justin was listed, but I knew that was a long shot. I might do better if I got on the Internet and used one of those online phone directories. That way I could include a bigger area than what was in the local book. Then if I did find him I could either call him or go over to his house.

I decided I'd try that plan first, and if it didn't pan out then I'd think of another approach. Like Jonathan used to tell me, there's always more than one way to tackle a cat. He was such a goofball.

"May I help you, sir?" the ticket woman asked me. The line had moved up while my mind was drifting, and the question startled me. I don't remember anybody ever calling me "sir" before. I guess she was just mouthing words she had to say to everybody, but it still felt weird.

"Oh, yeah. I need a ticket to Sulphur Springs, Texas, please," I told her. She fiddled around and typed something on her computer, not paying me any more mind.

"One way or round trip?" she asked.

"Just one way please," I said. She typed a little more.

"That will be forty-six dollars and fifty cents. How will you be paying today, sir?" she asked. I reached into my pocket and pulled out four tens and two fives and laid them on the counter. They were a little crumpled from being in my pocket.

"Oh, I'm sorry sir, we can't accept cash at this location. Do you have a credit or debit card?" she asked. This was a problem I hadn't thought of.

"Uh, no. . . Isn't there any way you could take cash just this once?" I asked.

"No, I'm afraid there's no way we can do that, sir. We can only accept credit or debit cards at this location," she said. I swear that woman must have been a robot. It sure was a lot like talking to one. I might as well have been arguing with a fence post.

I went and sat down on one of the benches in the terminal to think, and I guess I must have looked lost. I wouldn't have been surprised if I did.

"Is something wrong?" the lady beside me asked. She was a middle-aged woman in a long flowery dress who looked like she needed to lose a few pounds. You know the type. The ones who read romance novels and eat chocolate all the time, and always want to pinch your cheeks.

"I need to buy a ticket to get home, and the girl at the counter won't take cash," I said, truthfully enough.

"Your mom doesn't have a credit card?" she asked.

That was a dangerous question, because I certainly didn't want to get into an explanation of why I was trying to buy a ticket with cash. At least not a true one. I thought fast.

"I'm going home from my dad's house. He gave me the money for the ticket and dropped me off cause he was in a hurry, and I can't get ahold of him or my mom either one, and now I don't know what to do," I said smoothly. I was also lying through my teeth, and I felt pretty cruddy about that. The woman looked disgusted.

"That's just like a man, to not think of something like that," she declared, "Where do you live, honey?"

I almost laughed, but it would have blown everything if I had, so I bit my tongue to keep from it.

"Sulphur Springs, Texas," I told her meekly, trying to look as pitiful and helpless as I could. It must have worked, too.

"Well I think we can take care of that. I tell you what I'll do. I'll buy your ticket for you with my credit card, and then you can just pay me back with cash. How would that work?" she offered.

That was exactly what I was hoping she'd say, and I gave her the sweetest smile I knew how to make. Mama always used to say I could look like an angel when I was up to no good, and for once I really hoped she was right about that.

"Would you? I'd really appreciate that, ma'am," I told her, oozing with gratitude.

"Why of course I will, baby," she said, and she walked right up to the ticket counter and bought it for me with her MasterCard.

I gave her the cash, and I let her pat my head and kiss my cheek and buy me a Coke and do all those other things middle-aged ladies like to do to you for some reason. I knew it was coming, but I figured I owed her that much. She left pink lipstick on my cheek and that really grossed me out, but I resisted the urge to wipe the kiss away until after she was out of sight.

There are some good people in the world like that. I don't know how I would have got that ticket without her. I never did know that lady's name, but wherever she is today I wish her well.

After she disappeared I looked down at my ticket and noticed that I'd have to wait till eleven o'clock that night before the bus left. It was barely five-thirty at the time, so I sat on a bench in the terminal and killed a few hours reading my book. It's one of the best ways to keep people from talking to you. I'm not shy or unfriendly or anything, but I knew better than to talk to any more people than I had to. The more I talked, the more chance I had of slipping up and saying something wrong to somebody who didn't need to hear it, and the more people there would be who might remember me later if somebody came nosing around asking about me. That kind of thing was exactly what would get me caught and sent home if I wasn't careful. I had to be *smoke*, invisible as a fly on the wall.

So I drank my Coke the lady bought me and ate a couple of Twix bars from my food stash and waited till it was time for the bus to leave.

Sitting around twiddling your thumbs is no fun. There wasn't even a TV in that danged bus terminal. I spent about thirty minutes in the lavatory and did my best to wash a little bit of the grime and dirt off my body. I got a wad of paper towels and wetted them down and washed my face and my hands and my neck, and also behind my ears and under my arms. Then I rinsed my hair under the faucet and shook it as dry as I could, like a dog scattering water everywhere after it gets its fur wet. I tried drying it with the paper towels, but they just fell to pieces and left little bits of paper all in my hair. It wasn't much of a bath, but it was a whole lot better than nothing. I felt much better when I was done.

Then I went back outside and waited some more. My hair kept dripping down the back of my neck for the longest time, till it finally dried. I thought eleven o'clock would never come.

There was just one more little thing that happened while I was in Fort Smith. I barely paid attention at the time, but since it turned out to be important later on I guess I better tell you about it.

It was maybe ten o'clock, and I was half dead with boredom by that time. There was a boy across the aisle from me, signed into Yahoo Messenger on his cell phone. I knew that's what it was because he had the volume turned up real loud and I recognized the little beeps and sounds it made, cause Mama is addicted to Messenger. She talks to people on there all the time. Usually it's late at night, after Lola goes to bed, but I'd heard those sounds more times than I could remember. She even signed me up for an account here awhile back, but I hadn't thought about it in months.

After a while the boy got up and walked away, still wrapped up in his messaging, and at the time I thought no more about it. But later I was glad he reminded me.

When I got on the bus I sat by myself and asked for a blanket and a pillow. The bus was a lot more comfortable than the septic tank, and a whole lot warmer. Honestly though, I was so tired from raking yards all day that I probably could have slept on a park bench and thought it was heaven.

I did stay awake for a little while, looking out the window. You couldn't see much except the dark silvery outlines of tree-covered mountains against the sky, and some little farms and things scattered on the valley floors. It reminded me of Tennessee. After about an hour or so I got tired of looking at scenery, and I laid my head back and closed my eyes.

I drifted off to sleep, and not long after that I had a horrible nightmare.

I dreamed I was out in the woods by myself, and there were wolves chasing me to tear me to pieces. It had that fuzzy, unreal kind of flavor that dreams sometimes have, but that only made it worse. I ran and ran, but they were always coming closer, and I finally felt myself knocked down from behind by a snarling monster.

I guess he ate me. I'm not really sure, because I snapped awake right then, breathing hard and with my heart beating fast. I used to have nightmares like that when I was really little, but it had been years since it happened. It was weird to be having one again now.

"Bad dream?" the kid sitting next to me asked. He hadn't been there when I went to sleep, so I guess he either got on the bus later or else changed seats. He was about my age I guess, but taller and thinner. One of those bean pole types that looks almost like he could walk through a picket fence without opening the gate.

"Yeah, I was dreaming about monsters chasing me," I told him. I realized how stupid that sounded even while I was saying it, but it was too late to take it back. The other kid smiled a little, but at least he didn't laugh at me.

"Musta been a bad one then, cause you thrashed around an awful lot," he said.

Dreams are awful hard to remember, and I'd already almost forgotten most of what happened. When he said that, it reminded me how bad it had really been, and I wished he hadn't.

I wonder sometimes if dreams mean anything. I've always heard you could dream about stuff that hasn't happened yet, and that's always what scared me more than anything about nightmares. Especially that one I had on the bus. Because I knew there were really such things as monsters in the world, even if this other kid didn't.

All that ran through my head in just a second or two, but I didn't say anything about what I was thinking. He didn't need to know all that.

"Yeah, I guess it was," I finally said.

"Well hey, my name is Jonathan. Nice to meet you," he told me.

"I'm Zach. I used to have a friend named Jonathan," I said, realizing all of a sudden that I'd probably never see him again.

I guess I hadn't thought about it till then, but it wasn't just my family I gave up when I ran away, it was my friends and my home and a hundred other things too.

That stung more than I liked to admit, cause me and Jonathan had been best buds for as long as I could remember, and I hadn't even told him good-bye.

"Where you from, Zach?" the new Jonathan asked. We were getting onto territory I didn't want to talk about if I could help it, but I'd already told one brazen lie this evening and I didn't want to do it again.

"Aw, I'm from Tennessee. What about you?" I asked him, trying to turn the conversation away from me.

"I'm from Gillham, just down the road a little bit. I won't be on the bus much longer. I'm just comin' back home from visiting my sister," he said. He probably expected me to tell him where I'd been and what I was doing, but I didn't take the bait.

He didn't seem to notice, though. He started telling me a long, drawn-out story about his cousin riding a horse to school last winter when the roads were icy and how he tied it up to a tree in the parking lot. It sounded like something I would do. . . if I had a horse, that is. I'd been wanting one for a long time, but Daddy always said maybe someday.

I smiled and nodded and let Jonathan talk as long as he wanted to, which seemed to be a lot. He talked almost nonstop until the bus stopped in Gillham to let him off.

He wanted to trade addresses and phone numbers and stuff like that, and maybe I would have any other time. But as it was, I honestly didn't know what to tell him for either of those things. I told him I was moving and didn't know my address or phone number yet, but I'm not sure he believed me. He did give me his information. I think I've still got it in my billfold somewhere, maybe.

I liked the boy, but truthfully I was glad when he left. He was a chatterbox and I was ready to go back to sleep if I could. Maybe we could have been friends if we'd met some other place and time, but not right then.

I've never seen him again since.

Before long I went back to sleep, and as far as I know I didn't have any more bad dreams that night. Or if I did, then I don't remember them.

I was sound asleep when we crossed into Texas, so I missed my first glimpse of it. That kinda disappointed me. I woke up when we were about forty miles from the border, just about to cross the Sulphur River.

We passed through three or four more little towns I don't remember, and maybe it wouldn't have taken so long if we hadn't had to stop in every last single one of them. We stopped for nearly an hour in Mount Pleasant just for breakfast. I do remember that one, because the first thing I saw when we came into town was a billboard of a cowgirl holding up a big plate of cheesecake and saying "Welcome, Y'all!" I was hungry at the time and cheesecake sounded pretty darned good right then.

I knew I better save my cash though, so I ate a candy bar and an apple sitting outside on a bench in front of the restaurant, cause the driver wouldn't let us stay on the bus while he wasn't there.

It was still early, and I could see dew glistening like diamond dust on the leaves of the oak trees that bordered the parking lot. The sun was really bright that morning, and I had to shade my eyes with my hand to keep from squinting. I try never to squint because Nana told me your eyes can get stuck that way and never come loose. I'm pretty sure that's not true, but why take any chances?

Not long after breakfast the bus pulled into Sulphur Springs.

Chapter Five

It was about mid-morning when we got to the bus station, and that suited me just fine. It was a bright, coolish kind of day, with showers of yellow leaves coming down off the sweet gum trees whenever the wind blew. A good day for walking, and that was a fine thing. I found out you had to do a lot of walking in Sulphur Springs if you wanted to get anywhere. Everything is so sprawled out and far-flung it takes forever to get around if you don't have a car.

They had some of those free city maps that the Chamber of Commerce puts out, so I took one before I left the bus station.

I made my way to the public library, intending to follow my plan of getting on the Internet and seeing what I could find out. I'd come as far as I could with what I already knew, and now I needed some more information. I was in Daddy's home town, and I was hoping and praying Justin wasn't too far away. If he was, I didn't know what I might do.

But you know what? When I got there the dadgummed place was closed. I should have remembered it was Sunday. So many things had been going on the past couple of days that I just didn't think about it, I guess.

That left me out of luck as far as using the Internet. I wouldn't be able to do that until the library opened back up tomorrow morning, and in the meantime I had a whole day with nothing to do.

I don't know why I did it, but for some reason I walked over to Stonewall Street and looked at the houses. Curiosity, I guess. I didn't actually know which one Daddy and Nana Maralyn used to live in. They never mentioned any address that I could remember, and I'm sure I must have walked right past their old house that afternoon without knowing it. It gave me a weird feeling, to think about my dad growing up on that street and maybe playing in one of those very yards I was looking at when he was a kid.

It had always been a sort of unwritten rule in our family that nobody talked about the time before they became monsters or discussed any family members who weren't one. It was almost like it was taboo or something. I'd never paid attention or cared much before, but now, standing on that street, I decided I did care.

There were so many things nobody ever told me. I didn't know my grandparents (well, except for Nana Maralyn), or whether I had any aunts and uncles or cousins, or anything at all like that. Justin was the only family member I'd ever even heard of, and pretty much all I knew about him was a name and a face. Everybody else in the world knew all that stuff about where they came from, and I wanted to know too.

Maybe it seems like it was a strange time for me to want to get all balled up in family history when I was in such a tight spot in so many other ways. You'd think I'd have more practical things on my mind right then, like what to eat and where I could sleep that night. I don't know why it came over me all of a sudden like that, all this wondering about things I never thought about before.

A little kid was playing t-ball in one of the yards, and I watched him for a little while. Daddy used to be a fast pitch all-star in high school, and he could still throw pretty good when he wanted to.

When I was little, he used to play ball with me in the back yard sometimes, and I remember I always used to wish I could pitch as well as he could. So I practiced and I practiced till I learned how, and I'm not half bad these days if I do say so myself. Baseball used to be one of those things he and I could always talk about, till he decided it wasn't something he cared about anymore. I'm not sure exactly when that was, but for the past several years we hadn't done much together at all. He wanted to talk about money and monster stuff and I wanted to talk about baseball and books, and so we ended up barely talking at all.

When I thought about it, Mama was the same way, though. She just had different reasons. Lola was her whole world, and even though she did make an effort to hide it and be fair, everybody always knew who her favorite was. After my sister was born, she wasn't much interested in me anymore.

Neither of them were. Not really. They looked forward to me joining them in all their monster stuff, but that was only because that was what *they* cared about. I got the feeling they didn't really value anything I thought was important and didn't much care how I felt about things. It was almost like any other boy in the world would have done just as well to fill my place. That bites, you know.

I stood there feeling sorry for myself and wallowing in my unlovability for a while until I decided I was being stupid about the whole thing. I'd known all this stuff for years, so why was it all of a sudden upsetting me now? It wasn't like me to get all bummed out like that, and I don't know what put me in such a bad mood that day. Maybe it was just the place I was in, and all that broody thinking I was doing.

I decided to put it out of my mind.

I didn't stay on Stonewall Street much longer. It was too depressing and made me think too much. If I'd known it would do all that to me I never would have gone there in the first place. It was a headache I didn't need right then.

I eased my way back downtown, walking slowly with my thumbs hooked in the corners of my pockets. I went to a Taco Bell not far from the interstate and had a bean burrito for a dollar. It was nasty, but at least it was cheap.

I wandered around aimlessly the rest of that day. I looked in store windows, and fed the pigeons with some popcorn I bought. Yeah, I know it was probably a waste of money, but I did eat some of it myself. I was still in that funky mood from earlier, and sharing with the birds cheered me up a little.

Lots of places had their Christmas decorations up already, and when it started to get dark I enjoyed looking at lights and things for a while. But in a way that was depressing too, because it only reminded me I wasn't home.

It was the full moon that night, too. I could tell before it even got quite over the treetops. Mama and Daddy and

Nana would all be out hunting tonight, cause you could bet your beefcakes they wouldn't miss *that* for all the cows in Texas. And if I'd been home, then I would have been right out there with them, and that would have been my last night not a monster. I shivered.

I was careful not even to step on a bug or swat a fly that whole night. I wasn't sure what was big enough to count as making a kill, and I wasn't taking any chances. I had no intention of getting turned into a monster *now*, just because I was careless.

Later on I had to think of a place to spend the night again. You know, one of the most annoying things about running away is that you can never find a good place to sleep. I went back to the bus station and slept on a bench that particular night. At least it stays open twenty-four hours and nobody thinks it's very strange if you're sleeping there. It's also noisy, bright, and full of people all the time, and I swear the bus company must have tried every kind of bench in America before they found the very hardest and most uncomfortable kind possible. It was worse than gym bleachers.

When I woke up Monday morning the first thing I did was look at my fingernails. Mama and Daddy and Nana all have really hard, sharp nails even on ordinary days, almost like claws, and Nana had told me once that that was a good way to recognize a *loup-garou* when you saw one. You can bet I looked real close that morning, and except for a little dirt my fingernails looked just the same as they always had. That was a huge relief. Now at least I knew I'd be safe till next fall, even if I did get caught. For a little while, I was sky-high with excitement.

I jumped up and went back to the library not long after it opened, eager to get started. I guess I was still pumped up over dodging the bullet on getting turned into a *loup-garou,* but it didn't take long to bring me back down to reality.

All the public computers were busy when I got there (of course!), so I had to cool my heels in the lobby and wait for one. I finished reading *Robinson Crusoe* while I waited. I was almost done anyway, and when I finished I put it back in my pack. I really didn't like the ending much.

I still had to wait a while even after that, so I read the newspaper. Finally there was a vacant computer, and I sat down and got to work.

Like I said before, I had no idea where to find Justin except somewhere in Texas, and hopefully somewhere near Sulphur Springs. I knew it was probably too much to hope for that he was still there, but you never can tell about things like that. I was fairly close to Dallas, and there are lots of people there.

To tell the truth, I kind of hoped he didn't live in a big city. I like the wild places too much for that. But at the time I cared more about finding him at all than I did about what kind of place he lived in. I wouldn't have cared if he lived in a pup tent on a vacant lot. Well, maybe I would have cared about *that,* but you know what I mean.

I went to a website that had all the phone book listings in the country on it and tried to see what I could find. Even limiting the search to Texas, there were twenty-two Justin Wilders or JJ Wilders and so forth. I didn't know Justin's middle initial, so I couldn't cross out all the JR's and JB's and JT's and all that crud.

For a while I got discouraged, but then I took a piece of scratch paper and a pencil and started writing them all down. It would have cost me ten cents a page to print that stuff, and I couldn't afford it.

I had a horrible thought while I was writing down those names and phone numbers. What if Justin was married and the phone was listed under his wife's name? What if he only had a cell phone, or no phone at all? Worst of all, what if he moved away ten years ago and was living nine hundred gazillion miles from here?

I finally decided there was nothing I could do about any of that, so I'd better work on what I had before I started worrying about what to do if none of those people turned out to be the right one. You can't always be worrying about what *might* happen. The stuff you already have to deal with is hard enough.

It would have been easiest if I could have just called all those guys and asked them a few questions. But I didn't have a phone, and it would have cost way too much to try to do all that on a payphone. So I had to tackle that cat a little bit different kind of way if I wanted to get anything done.

I used Google and came up with some personal websites for several Justin Wilders. I was able to cross out three of the people on my phone number list that way because I found out things about them that meant they couldn't be the one I was looking for. Two of them were too old, and one of them had posted a picture of himself that looked nothing like Justin at all.

It might sound like I was making progress in whittling down the number of people I had to check out, but even though I was able to cross out a few, I also had to add five more people I found on Google that I hadn't seen on the phone book site. It was enough to drive me crazy. It also made me wonder how many others I might be missing because I didn't know where to look for them.

It would be dull to tell you about everything I looked at that afternoon, cause I was there till they closed that night at ten. In the end I wound up with a list of people that had twelve names on it of people that might possibly be Justin. One in Amarillo, two in Dallas, one in Tyler, three in Houston, one in Lufkin, one in Daingerfield, one in Mineral Wells, one in New Boston, and the last one in Wolfe City.

I didn't know where any of those places were except Dallas and Houston, so I had to haul out a Texas road map and fiddle around until I found them all.

I sort of wondered about the Wolfe City one, and if maybe Justin had a sense of humor. It sounded like the kind of place a werewolf might want to live.

Except Justin wasn't one, of course. I guess for a minute I sorta forgot that was the whole reason for finding him in the first place.

I noticed that most of those towns were in the eastern or northeastern part of the state, and that was a good thing. None of them were what you might call close. But it was a heck of a lot better than having them scattered everywhere. Wolfe City was the closest, and it was about thirty-five miles away. None of the others were closer than sixty miles.

After the library closed, I spent one more night at the bus station. I knew if I spent too many nights in there somebody would start to notice after awhile, so I tried to make myself as inconspicuous as possible. I slept in a corner away from the ticket counter where it was hard to see me and not too many people had any reason to come.

I used up the last of my food that night. I ate my last piece of beef jerky and the last can of Beanie Weenies. I still had a little money, but precious little, and I knew it wouldn't last long at all if I started buying food with it.

Tuesday morning I went back to the library and tried to see if I could find out any more about the people I was looking at, any little clues that might help me. No such luck, though, and I didn't know any other websites to check.

I finally decided I'd just have to bite the bullet and use a payphone to check out the rest of them, in spite of the cost. It was a dollar apiece for every call, and that would eat up the rest of my money real fast.

I decided it was probably wise to check out the closest ones first, but what could I ask these people when I called? I was afraid if I just came right out and told them who I was and what I was looking for, they wouldn't believe me. The only proof I had was that picture I got from Mama's album, and I couldn't show them that over the phone. Mama hated talking about Justin so much, what if he was the same way? He might not admit he even had a sister, even if I asked about her by name.

Maybe it sounds like I was being a worry-wart, but things start not being very funny when you're completely alone and almost a thousand miles from home, in a place where you don't know anybody. I never realized how scary and lonely it could be.

I started feeling sorry for myself again, and I almost decided to give up and go home, tell everybody I was sorry and start eating bloody rabbits once in a while.

It's bad when you get so sick at heart that you start thinking about stuff like that. I'm not sure what kept me from doing it. All I know is, I felt like somewhere deep down, somebody was reminding me to have courage.

So after a while I did, and I decided not to give up at least until I didn't have any choice. One of my teachers used to talk about guardian angels sometimes. Maybe it was something like that.

Anyway, I went outside to a payphone and started calling those numbers. I'd decided there was really nothing else I could say except the honest truth, and hope things worked out.

Wolfe City was first on the list, but as it turned out, when I called that number all I got was message telling me it was disconnected. That was good in a way since I didn't get charged for the call, but it didn't give me much information either. So I moved on to the next one.

Neither of the Dallas guys was the right person. One of them was nice enough; he just told me he wasn't who I was looking for and wished me good luck. The other one was ruder about it but he said basically the same thing.

Out of the other nine, I got five answering machines, two more disconnected numbers, and two more people who turned out not to be the right one. Those two were the ones in Tyler and Mineral Wells.

It's awfully hard to tell much about a person just from hearing his voice on an answering machine. Some people don't even bother to say anything themselves, and others seem to want to talk your ear off before they'll even let you leave your message. But sometimes you can tell a little bit. I figured out that two of the people in Houston were black, the one in Lufkin was older than dirt, and the one in Amarillo was a foreigner, so that eliminated four more possibilities.

One of the disconnected numbers was in Houston, and the other was in Daingerfield. The number in New Boston just rang and rang, so I bet he probably didn't have an answering machine at all. Most everybody does nowadays, so it made me think maybe that one was a really old guy too.

I drummed my fingers on the phone and thought some more. The one number that I knew was working was in New Boston, which was maybe eighty miles away. Two of the disconnected ones were pretty close too, even though they were in opposite directions.

I knew I couldn't automatically cross out a number just because it was disconnected. Not unless I knew what the reason was. They might just have forgot to pay their bill last month or something. I didn't dare eliminate the numbers unless I knew for sure. So that left me with four numbers to check on: Wolfe City, Daingerfield, New Boston, and Houston.

When all the water was boiled out of the pot, the real question at that point was how to get to any of these places. I'd found out everything I could without actually going to the address itself to see it with my own eyes.

The hardest would be that one in Houston because it was so far away, so I decided to put that one off till last. The other three were not too awful far.

The problem was, I'd spent almost all the rest of my money making those phone calls. I had not quite three dollars left, and that won't get you too far.

Chapter Six

As it turned out, I had to spend more than two weeks in Sulphur Springs. The rest of that Tuesday and most of the rest of the time I was there I spent working my tail off to make some money. There weren't nearly so many yards that needed raking as there had been in Fort Smith, but I mowed some grass, and picked up trash, and swept parking lots, and did some other odd jobs like that.

People will usually let a kid do something for them, if you ask them the right way. I learned that from my dog. He wasn't supposed to eat food off the table, but he could look at you with such pitiful eyes that you'd give in sooner or later and let him have a little bit. I figured if it worked on me, then it ought to work on other people. So I made sure to look extra pitiful whenever I went up to anybody's house. It wasn't such a hard thing to do, under the circumstances.

I had to be careful not to look *too* pathetic, though, because then people start asking questions about where you live and stuff like that. Things I definitely didn't want to answer.

I did have one little piece of luck early on, though. Some people paid me thirty bucks on Tuesday afternoon to clean out their garage, and they told me I could keep anything I found in there that I wanted. There was a bunch of things I might have wanted if I'd had anywhere to put the stuff, but the only things I ended up taking were some clothes that fit me, a little box of assorted tools, a few books, and an old BMX bicycle.

The bike was the real prize. It had two flat tires and a rusty chain, and it was beat up and scratched and ugly as sin. Somebody had tried to paint it black with a spray can, and then they'd painted the words "The Beast" on the crossbar with what looked like red fingernail polish. They even put little drippy things under the letters to make them look like blood. I thought that was sorta cool.

It didn't look like much, to be sure, but everything worked okay. The bearings were tight and except for the chain it didn't have much rust on it. I had to get new tubes for the tires and a new chain, but that stuff didn't cost much. I had the old beast fixed up in less than an hour, and then I had a lot faster way to get around town than walking. You'd be amazed how much difference it made. The little tool kit had everything in it that I needed.

I found two pairs of jeans and three black t-shirts that were a little too big for me. They looked like concert t-shirts, because they had *Poison* and *Metallica* and *Def Leppard* on them. They were old and musty and a little holey, but not so much that I couldn't still get some use out of them for a while. There was a black jacket so big it hung down almost to my knees, but I took that too. Those people really liked black stuff, as much as they had of it.

I didn't dare keep sleeping in the bus station anymore, so I bought me a sleeping bag at Wal-Mart for ten bucks at the same time I got the tubes and chain for The Beast, and then I started sleeping in that. It was warm enough to keep me from freezing outside.

That night I slept under a little bridge where the highway crossed a dry creek bed at the edge of town. But I didn't like that very much. It didn't stop the wind from blowing right in my face, and the sound of cars passing by over your head isn't a very nice thing to listen to all night long. Worst of all, anybody who looked very close could see that I was there. I decided after just one night that that would never do, and Wednesday morning I started out to look for something better if I could find anything.

I was riding The Beast over on the north side of town when I passed a big vacant lot, all grown up in trees and thickets and heavy grass. I looked it over a bit and thought it might have some thick bushes I could crawl up under that would probably be a better place to sleep than under the bridge. It would at least block the wind and be a lot more private.

I wormed my way in there and found the remains of an old burnt down house. That didn't interest me too much, but when I elbowed my way into the back yard I struck pure gold. There was a big home-made dog house back there, almost hidden amongst the weeds. It was maybe eight foot square and four feet high, with a wooden floor up off the ground and a shingled roof. I'm betting it was for a Rottweiler or a Mastiff or some other bigger kinda dog like that. Whatever it used to be for, it suited me just fine.

It had been empty for a long time, so it wasn't nasty or anything. I could still smell dog a little bit when I crawled inside, and there was some old musty dirty straw that I had to throw out. But once I did that, I had a place to sleep that was warm and dry where nobody would ever think to find me, and at that point that's all I cared about.

I took to leaving my sleeping bag and my backpack inside the dog house every day, so I wouldn't have to carry them while I was raking leaves and working.

I fixed the place up pretty nice as time went by. One of the first things I did was to get a piece of plywood for a door. I went to the lumber yard and got them to give me a piece of scrap wood for that, and they even cut it the right size for me. They weren't too busy on a Wednesday afternoon and I guess they probably thought I was building a tree house or something like that, so they were willing to be nice about it. They didn't even charge me for it.

I rummaged around in the burnt out house till I found some screws and hinges, and I bought a cheap hasp and padlock set so I could keep the place locked up. I put it on with the screwdriver from my tool kit, and then I had a door. I got a little thing of cherry air freshener to kill the musty dog smell, and I hauled some fresh hay in there to make me a softer place to sleep. I even found a little oil lamp for fifty cents at a yard sale so I had lights after dark if I wanted to read. It wasn't half bad.

It sounds weird, I guess, but I was really proud of myself for having my own little house, if you want to call it that. It wasn't much, but at least it was mine and it was more than some people had. It was much nicer than a tent, and I'd never minded living in one of those for a week or two when I went camping in the summer.

Maybe that just shows how poor and pitiful I really was by then, but like I said, I don't think it was *that* terrible. I came home every evening about dark, lit my lamp for a little while and read one of my books till I got sleepy, then I blew out the light and got up again in the morning and went roaming on The Beast looking for another odd job to do. Sometimes I found one and sometimes I didn't.

I brought water home from the car wash down the street in an empty milk jug I snatched from a trash can, and I tried to at least wash the parts of me that showed, if not every night then at least every other night. I would have dearly loved a shower, but you do what you have to do.

It rained on Friday, so I had to stay inside all day long that day. There wasn't much to do besides read my books and listen to the sound of rain hitting the roof. It didn't leak, and the walls shut off the wind. Other than being a little cold I really couldn't complain, and I just wrapped up in my sleeping bag and snuggled a little deeper into the hay. I was reading *A Wrinkle in Time*, which was one of the books I found in that garage I cleaned out.

I listened to my radio for a little bit at lunch time, mostly to hear the weather. I had a box of crackers and a spray can of Easy Cheese there in the dog house that I kept for emergencies like that, so I didn't have to go out in the rain to find anything to eat. I wouldn't have wanted to leave fresh tracks in the mud anyway.

I had to be careful that I didn't beat a trail through the weeds even on dry days, so I always went in a different way each time to keep from leaving any signs I was there. I might be fairly comfortable now, but I didn't dare forget I was still hiding.

Things were fairly tolerable for the time being, but when I stopped to think about it I knew I was just frittering away time and not getting much done except just barely surviving. It's easy to forget that, when you're so busy trying to live from day to day, but when I laid awake at night on my straw tick, I had plenty of time to think.

I was having to spend almost all the money I made just to buy food. I ate greasy fried chicken and corn dogs and tater logs out of those hot boxes at convenience stores. I had a lot of those nasty bean burritos at Taco Bell, and whatever I could find on the dollar menu anywhere else. You can survive on less than ten bucks a day if you really have to, but sometimes I didn't make that much. Leaf raking season was pretty much over and done with, and jobs were starting to get scarce.

Worse than that, I knew sooner or later somebody would notice that I wasn't in school when I was supposed to be, or they'd see me slipping in and out of the thicket where my shed was. It was only a matter of time before something like that happened.

I wasn't too much afraid of anybody trying to hurt me, cause I think I can hold my own in a fight if I had to. I was more afraid of busybodies. There are all kinds of people out there who think they're doing you a favor by meddling in your business. People like that wouldn't see how much I'd done. They'd see a twelve year old boy in dirty clothes living in a dog house all alone in the winter and raking yards so he could have money to eat, and they'd feel like it was their duty to "help" me by sending me home. They wouldn't care a bit that they might be sending me back to something worse than where I was at, and they wouldn't believe me if I told them why. Those were the kind of people I had to stay away from no matter what happened.

I was having a hard time deciding which of those places I found on the Internet that I should check first, because I knew a wrong choice could put me in a really bad situation. I'd just now managed to arrange things so I was barely getting along by the skin of my teeth. What if I got to New Boston, or Daingerfield, or Wolfe City, and it turned out that wasn't where the right Justin lived? How would I get the money or have the time to check the other ones? Or even to get back to Sulphur Springs?

To make things worse, winter was coming on fast, and I promise you it can get bitter cold at night, even in Texas. Right now I was at least sheltered and safe to sleep at night, I had a locked door and a home of some kind, and if I left Sulphur Springs I'd be right back to being homeless and on the mercy of the world. I didn't like that feeling at all, and in a lot of ways it just seemed safer to sit tight where I was, even though I knew I couldn't do that forever, or even for much longer. Pretty soon there wouldn't be any more yards to rake, and then what would I do?

If you want the honest truth, I was afraid, and I had pretty good reason to be. I was afraid to leave and I was afraid not to.

Nobody ever taught me how to pray. It wasn't something we ever did at home. But I'd always heard there was a God, and I thought it couldn't hurt to ask Him to show me the right way to go. I sure didn't have anybody else to ask at the time. So that's what I did, right there in my little shed in Sulphur Springs, on Sunday night two weeks after I first rolled into town. I didn't know if He heard me or not.

When I woke up the next morning, I decided to head for Wolfe City. Partly because it was closest, and partly because, oh, I don't know, it just seemed like the right choice to make. Maybe it was God answering my prayer, or maybe it was something else. Sometimes you do things without really knowing why.

I locked up the shed and kept my key, just in case I ever needed to come back, and I hid The Beast under some burnt wood and trash from the old house. Then I walked down to the carwash and started chatting with anybody that looked friendly. It's the best way to get a ride. People don't always like to stop for you on the side of the road, but if they're washing their car they don't have any choice but to listen to you. If you seem friendly enough then sometimes they'll do you a favor.

I ended up hitching a ride with a high school kid who took me as far as Cumby. That was only ten miles or so, but it was the best I could do. I had to pay him ten bucks to take me, but other than that he was nice enough. I didn't gripe about it, even though my cash was running really low again. There are times when you just don't have a choice, and I probably stank enough that he deserved ten bucks for putting up with me.

You never notice things like that yourself, but it had been two and a half weeks since I had a real shower and it wouldn't have surprised me that I was getting pretty ripe.

He dropped me off at a convenience store downtown, if you could call it that. Cumby was too small to have much of a downtown.

Anyway, I had a map, and since I didn't have any other way to get where I was going, I decided I'd just have to walk the rest of the way unless somebody was nice enough to pick me up. If it took me two or three days, it wouldn't matter much. I was used to sleeping in uncomfortable places by then, and I had my sleeping bag to keep me warm.

Mama used to say the job you never start is the one that takes the longest to finish, so I took a deep breath and got started. I walked north up the main street for a little while, then turned left by a big house for a few blocks and then right again at the First Baptist Church. After that it wasn't long till I was out of town. Like I said, Cumby isn't a very big place.

It was the first time I'd actually been out in the country since I left home, because you couldn't count while I was inside the septic tank or on the bus. There wasn't really much to say about the countryside as I went along, just a bunch of rolling pasture land with some clumps of little trees here and there and along the fence rows. It wasn't like Tennessee, but it was pretty in its own way.

Just being back out in the country cheered me up a lot, and for the first time in days I wished I had somebody to talk to. It was just me and bunches of cows, though, and they don't talk much. Oh, and lots of big round hay bales, too, but they talk even less than the cows.

I walked all day to get to Commerce, and my good mood gradually wore off. I was a little disgusted that nobody stopped to give me a ride. It was eleven miles from Cumby to Commerce, and I was bone tired by the time I made it into town late that afternoon. My feet were numb from walking, and where they weren't numb they ached. I wasn't used to doing that much leg work in such a short space of time.

I wished I could have brought The Beast with me. It would have made things a whole lot easier. But I hadn't, and eleven miles on foot is a lot farther than you think it is, I promise you. So I wasn't in the best mood I've ever been in, to say the least.

I saw a gas station coming up not far down the road, and when I got there I turned into the parking lot and went inside. I paid for a coke and sat down on one of the benches in the front of the store by the sliding glass doors. I closed my eyes and laid my head back against the cinder block wall, too tired to even move. It felt so good to get off my feet.

I think I must have dozed off for a while, because when I opened my eyes it was getting to be dusky outside. I was mad at myself for wasting time like that, but I was just so, so tired. I hadn't even opened my coke from earlier, so I twisted off the cap now and drank about half of it in several big gulps. I was still tired even after sleeping, and my muscles were stiff and sore, but I thought I could move on now for at least a little while. I'd have to find somewhere to spend the night before long. I missed my shed, just like I knew I would.

I trudged a little farther down the street, and before long I came in sight of some buildings that looked like a college campus. I figured that sounded like a promising place to go, cause there are always lots of kids in places like that and there tend to be people around pretty much all the time. After a little hunting I found the library, and it was a monster; five stories tall.

I breezed in like I owned the place and didn't even glance at the girl behind the circulation desk, just headed right on past her down the hall to the left. There were stairs that led to the upper levels, but I was hoping to find an elevator. I'd had about as much as my legs could take for a day.

I found the elevators before long and went all the way up to the fifth floor. It was quiet up there, with no students in sight. Just a lot of shelves of dusty books and some plastic couches and coffee tables. I always wondered why they put those in libraries, since I'm sure you're not supposed to drink anything in there. It seems like tables and chairs would work better for studying.

The only other features were a computerized card catalog station, and a water fountain that hummed quietly to itself by the elevators.

Almost the entire fifth floor was one big room, and there were these huge windows all around where you could look outside. I walked up to the closest one and looked out to the east, and it seemed like you could see forever. Texas looks dadgummed flat from that high up, I have to say. I didn't see a single hill, and for a second I was homesick for Tennessee. But I knew if I thought about that too much I'd drive myself batty.

Instead, I went over to the other bank of windows that looked west, to see if I could figure out where Wolfe City might be. I still had my map, so I knew about where it *should* be. I knew it was somewhere off to the northwest. I just wanted to see it with my own two eyes.

I looked down and found the main highway that ran through Commerce, and followed it with my eyes till it joined another big highway next to a McDonald's and a football stadium. The stadium was marked on my map, so I knew I had the right place. I followed the highway northwest for a while, as far as I could.

It got all hazy and blurry from the distance before long, and I couldn't have said for sure whether I was looking at Wolfe City or not. I knew it wasn't a very big town, and there were houses and things scattered pretty evenly all over the place. It was hard to tell if they were clumped up a little thicker in one place. I thought so, but I couldn't be sure. But then again it was fourteen miles away, so I might have been imagining things.

I turned away from the window, disappointed. I guess I hadn't realized how bad I wanted to see the place. You might think I was putting way too much hope in this one spot when Justin might not even live there. And maybe I was. But I'd been running for what felt like forever, even though I knew it wasn't even three weeks yet, and I'd already decided I didn't like it at all. I was ready to have it all be over.

Chapter Seven

That night I stayed in the library. It was a little bit risky, but I thought it was worth it to be able to stay someplace warm.

I waited until right before closing time, and then I went out onto the fire stairs and climbed up the steps that led to the roof. The roof door was locked, of course, but I hid up there as high as I could for about thirty minutes, like a bat in a cave. If anybody had come down the fire stairs and looked up there they probably couldn't have kept from seeing me, but luckily nobody did.

I waited until I was sure everybody was gone, and then I slipped back down the steps and through the door. The lights were off, but it wasn't hard to see because of all the windows.

A library looks really spooky in the dark, I have to say. If I had let myself think about it, I would have been imagining I saw all kinds of ghosts and bogies out of the corners of my eyes. I decided real quick that I better think about something else besides that.

I crossed the room and laid down on one of the plastic couches. It was already almost midnight, and I wasn't used to staying up that late. The whole time I'd been in my shed in Sulphur Springs, I hadn't stayed up more than two or three hours after dark, and this time of year that meant I'd been going to bed about eight thirty. So I was yawning my head off already.

I set the alarm on my watch to wake me up at six thirty in the morning so I could go hide again before they came to turn the lights on upstairs, and then I laid there for awhile with my hands behind my head and looked out through the windows and thought about things.

You couldn't see very many stars because of all the light from the town, and for some reason I missed that. In my room at home there was a window that looked out to the east, and sometimes on dark nights I used to leave my curtains open so I could pick out the stars I knew. I went through a phase where I was all into astronomy and stuff. I knew how to find a bunch of them. Aldebaran and Achernar, Antares and Canopus, Regulus and Vega, I knew all those and more. I thought it was so cool they all had their own names like that. It made them seem like people.

I think Sirius is my favorite star, though, because it's so bright and blue and because it's supposed to be called the Dog Star. I thought that was awesome, even though I didn't know why it had that name. I asked Nana one time, and she used to tell me it was because it was high in the sky in the hot summertime and it caused all the dogs to slobber in the water that time of year.

I don't know if that was true or not or where she heard such a thing, but I do remember being grossed out every time I saw a little bit of foam on the water at the swimming hole after that, cause I thought it was dog slobber and I didn't want to get any of it on me. It's funny what you remember sometimes, isn't it?

I couldn't see Sirius through the big window, though, so after awhile I gave up trying. I did find Achernar, still twinkling blue like he always had.

Watching the stars made me forget about spooks, and after a little while I closed my eyes. It was good to feel like I was back on the right track again, making some progress toward trying to find Justin and getting things settled for once and all.

That's the last thought I remember having before my alarm woke me up. It was still dark, and it seemed like the whole night had gone by in an eyeblink.

I was still nine tenths asleep and had this fuzzy idea I was in my own bed at home. I groaned a little bit and rolled over cause I didn't want to wake up that early.

I guess I probably would have gone right back to sleep again in spite of the alarm, cause I was just that dead beat, and if I had then I would have got caught red handed when the librarians came to turn the lights on.

Lucky for me though (well sort of) the couch was narrow and when I turned over I rolled right off and hit the concrete floor. My head and my right knee clipped the sharp edge of that darned coffee table on the way down, and you can bet your aunt's girdle that woke me up for sure.

I sat there on the floor rubbing my ear and my knee and wanting to kick that danged table. I'd bit my tongue too when I hit my head. You'd think they'd keep dangerous things like that away from public places, wouldn't you? I would, if it was up to me.

Anyway I didn't kick it cause I didn't want to make any noise. I just gave it a black look and hoped somebody chopped it up for firewood someday soon. Then I hobbled over to the east windows to see outside.

I say it was dark, but not completely. You could see the first streaks of light down low in the sky, even though it was too dark to read or anything yet. I was still groggy and not thinking too clearly, so I stood there in front of the window like an idiot for several minutes and didn't move. I was probably in plain view of anybody who happened to be outside on the lawn at such an uncivilized hour, if they happened to look up in just the right place.

As soon as it dawned on me what I was doing, I backed away from the window real quick and melted into the shadows amongst the books. You never just "go" into a shadow, you know, you always "melt" into one. I like that. It made me feel all sneaky and invisible, like nobody could possibly find me, and that's exactly the way I wanted it right then.

I shook the cobwebs out of my head and decided I had to get smarter than that, no matter how worn out I was. It scared me that I'd been so careless. It wasn't like me.

At least I hoped it wasn't.

Before long the lights came on, and I was extra specially careful to be completely quiet and still for a little while. I heard the door shut when the librarian left the room, but that didn't mean I was safe just yet. I had to wait for the library to actually open so nobody would wonder how I got in there.

I couldn't leave immediately even after that, because for a little while I knew they might remember who they'd seen walk through the doors that morning. I had to give them time to forget.

It wasn't hard though. As soon as the building was officially open, I walked right out in the open and sat down on the couch to read a book for a little while. I don't remember what it was; just something I picked off the shelf at random to make it look like I was doing something in case anybody came by and wondered why a kid was at the library on a Tuesday morning instead of in school.

Nobody did, so I guess it didn't much matter one way or the other. In fact nobody even came up to the top floor the whole time I was there. It was so quiet you could have heard a pencil hit the carpet, if anybody had dropped one.

When about an hour had gone by, I decided that was enough time. I got up and went downstairs to the first floor, and walked right past the circulation desk just as bold as brass. The lady was looking at her computer and didn't even glance at me when I walked out the door. So much for that!

It was a little frosty outside that morning in the patches where the sun hadn't managed to shine just yet, and the air was chilly. I stopped to put on my jacket before I went anywhere else, and when I pulled it out of my backpack even I noticed that it didn't smell too good in there. My clothes were starting to get pretty grubby and dirty, cause I hadn't had a chance to wash them all week. I couldn't afford it. I had to eat. The clothes I got from that garage in Sulphur Springs were never too clean to start with.

I hate being dirty. It makes people think you don't ever wash. Even when that's the truth, you still don't want people thinking it, do you?

There was no wind that morning, and nothing much to hear except a few birds in the trees and some traffic noise. The campus was deserted. I guess most of the students were in class right then, but for whatever reason I didn't see anybody.

It looked like it might turn out to be a really pretty day, and I would have enjoyed it more if my feet hadn't been so sore and I hadn't still been so tired and hungry. I nibbled on a devil's food cupcake that I got from a vending machine, but that was about all I could afford right then.

If you had asked me a month ago how I'd like it if I got to eat candy and cokes and junk food for every meal, I probably would have thought it was a great idea. But now it seemed a lot less appetizing. I would have given a lot for some real food right then. I wondered what Justin was having for breakfast that morning.

By and by I passed a pond with a fountain in the middle, and crossed over a busy street with four lanes of traffic. I spotted the football stadium, so I knew I was at the right intersection. I dreaded the idea of walking another fourteen miles, but at least I knew that was the last of it. You can put up with a lot of things, if you know they'll be over soon.

I can't really say much about the walk, except that it seemed to take forever. By the time I dragged myself into Wolfe City it was maybe an hour or so before dark, and my feet and legs were hurting so much I didn't think I could take even one more step. My whole body hurt. If you've ever been totally and completely exhausted then you know how I felt right then. I'd had as much walking as I ever wanted to do ever again in my life. I'd only *thought* yesterday was bad, but it was *nothing* compared to that second day of hiking.

I didn't let it knock me back, though. I told myself I was almost there and soon everything would be all right. I wanted to believe Justin was there in Wolfe City so bad I guess I convinced myself.

Because if he wasn't. . .

My only choice then would be to walk that whole thirty-five weary miles back to Sulphur Springs, and when I got there I'd be too sore and exhausted to do yard work for a few days at least. Then I'd have a choice between starving or rummaging in trash cans, and I couldn't decide which one would be worse.

I came to a little convenience store and mustered enough energy to go up to the counter and ask to borrow their phone book. Phone books are wonderful things, when you stop to think about it. Where else could you find so much information so fast?

I sat down and flipped my way through it, and sure enough, there was Justin Wilder listed. It gave his address as 392 Wild Buck Lane, wherever that was.

There was a big blown-up map of Hunt County on the wall by the door, so I went over to it and picked out Wolfe City first. Then I started combing through the surrounding area looking for that street name. I looked and looked until I was blue in the face, but I could *not* find the darned thing.

I finally gave up and decided to ask the clerk. She was a red-faced girl with orange hair who looked like she was bored, but I hoped maybe she might know where the dadgummed road was.

"Excuse me, miss, do you know where Wild Buck Lane is?" I asked her.

"Is that in Wolfe City, sugar?" she asked.

"Yeah, it's in the phone book but I can't find it on the map," I told her. She chewed her gum and thought about it.

"Naw, seems like I mighta heard of it before, but I don't remember where it's at," she finally said, "But that map on the wall is not too good. There are some better ones on the rack over there next to the Icee machine."

"Uh, thanks," I told her, and wandered over there to see what she was talking about.

I found the map stand, and it did indeed have some new county maps. They were that annoying kind that have the plastic wrap around them so you can't look at them without buying one. I swear, whoever thought of that idea ought to be shot first and then fed to the hogs.

The map cost two dollars, and that meant I had a choice between buying the map or getting something to eat that night. I had two dollars and thirty cents left in my pocket, and that was the last drop. Paying that kid for the ride to Cumby yesterday almost broke me.

The girl at the counter wasn't paying any attention, and for a second I was tempted to just take one of the maps and slip it up under my shirt and leave. When your back is up against a wall you start thinking about stuff like that. I don't remember ever stealing anything in my life and I really didn't want to try it now. I could imagine what Justin would say if the first time he ever saw me was when he had to come get me at the police station for shoplifting. What a great first impression *that* would make.

On the other hand, I was so hungry my head hurt. I hadn't had anything to eat all day except those two chocolate cupcakes early that morning. So I dithered and dawdled and couldn't make up my mind what to do.

In the end I decided not to take the map, since I know you're probably all on pins and needles wondering what happened. I know, I know, it sounds like a lot of build up for nothing, but it mattered a whole lot at the time.

I was reading a story once about a boy who got thrown out on the street in London or someplace like that, and I remember something an old man told him, that you never did wrong by doing right, no matter how hard it was at the time. I sure hoped he was right about that.

What I did do was buy myself a roasted hot dog smothered with so much mustard and chili and nacho cheese that it was dripping over the edge of the plastic container. It cost me ninety-nine cents, and I intended to get every penny worth. It was a self-serve kind of thing where you got your own bun and reached into the wiener-roaster with some tongs to get the one you wanted, then you got your own chili and cheese from a dispenser, however much or little you wanted.

I still had a little over a dollar left, so I got me an extra large Coke to go with it. I had no idea when my next meal might be, so I wanted this one to count.

I sat at a booth and attacked the food like I hadn't seen any in days. I got cheese and chili all over my chin and my fingers, but I didn't care. I licked them clean, and when I was done I licked the container clean. Laugh if you want to, but you've probably never been that hungry before. And if you have, then you know how it feels.

I killed the Coke with one last gulp, then sat there for a little bit resting my feet and relishing the feeling of being full. Then I went and got a free refill on my Coke and refilled my hot dog container with chili and cheese. I didn't have the money to get another dog, but a bowl of chili and cheese would suit me just fine, and there was a sign over the dispenser that said extra chili was just twenty-five cents. I could afford that. Barely.

I went in the bathroom and washed my hands and my face to get the cheese off, then I went back out to the map stand. I looked at those maps with a hangdog look on my face, I'm sure, because after a minute the orange haired girl came up behind me.

"You find the one you need?" she asked.

"Yeah, I think so, but it costs too much," I admitted, pointing to the map of Hunt County. She reached past me and picked one up.

"Well I don't guess it matters if you just look at it for a minute," she said. She tore the plastic off and handed me the map like it didn't matter a bit.

"Thanks," I told her. I wasn't sure what else to say, so I unfolded the new map and looked at the list of street names down in the bottom corner. Sure enough, there it was: Wild Buck Lane. I ran my fingers across the map to where it said the street should be, and found it. It wasn't long, just a little spike off the highway maybe a half mile west of town.

The thought of walking another half a mile was depressing, but I was so excited I finally knew where to find the place that I didn't care.

I folded the map back up and handed it to the girl, and she put it back on the rack without bothering to slip it inside the plastic jacket. I grabbed my Coke and my chili cheese and headed out the door with a smile on my face, sure that everything was almost over.

Chapter Eight

I'd like to be able to say things turned out the way I expected them to, but maybe that was too much to ask for.

I made it to the road just as it was getting dark outside, and I saw that it was a short street with several little white houses that were all pretty much the same. They weren't bad looking, but not particularly nice either. The ones near the highway were pretty close together, but the farther I went down the road the more straggled out they got, with big gaps and lots of trees in between them.

There were lights on in most of them, but nobody was outside. Just as well, I thought to myself. Number 392 was the last one on the street, where it petered out into a narrow dirt track that went on into the woods somewhere. It was a long way from the other houses, set way back in the thickets where you wouldn't have guessed it was even there unless you just knew.

I didn't see any lights on, but that was okay. I was ready to knock until I woke somebody up, or wait on the doorstep half the night if I had to, if nobody was home. I headed for it eagerly, just as fast as my sore feet would take me. It had a longish dirt driveway that cut back from the street, and the yard was kinda weedy and grown up, but I didn't pay much attention to that.

I finally came to the house itself, and when I did I got a nasty surprise. Tacked up on the front porch was a nice big red and white "For Sale" sign.

When I saw that, all my hopes suddenly came crashing down faster than a cat could lick its tail. I didn't realize till then how much faith I'd put in this one place, and having the rug yanked out from under my feet so fast like that was more than I knew how to take.

I sat down on the porch steps and cried for awhile. I know it was babyish and it didn't help, but I couldn't keep from it that night. I think that was the first time I ever cried since I broke my big toe playing football last summer.

After a little bit I shut off the waterworks and thought about what I should do next. There are times when you just don't feel like going on, but you still know you have to, and that was one of those times for me. The first thing I had to do was get back to Sulphur Springs and rest a few days at the shed and try to save up a little money if I could. There were still those other places to go check, New Boston and Daingerfield and so on.

I knew in my mind that there was no reason to give up just yet, but I was so tired, and so cold, and so grubby and broke and uncomfortable in other ways, the disappointment was hard to take right then.

I'd have to start out tomorrow and get back to the shed as fast as I could, but the most immediate thing to think about was what to do that very night. I could tell it was going to be a bitter cold one, because I could already see my breath in the air even that early. It wasn't the kind of night I needed to spend outside with no shelter, not even wrapped in a sleeping bag. I had nowhere to go and no money, and December is a cruel time of year to find yourself in that position.

I went up to the front door of the house and tried the knob. It was locked, like I halfway expected it would be. I figured I had nothing to lose, so I walked around to the back door and tried that one too. It was also locked, and I really wasn't in the mood to break in. I looked under the mat to see if there might be a key under there cause that's where we always kept our key at home, but there wasn't one.

There was a deck built on top of the garage with a door leading out onto it from the second floor of the house, and I wondered if that was locked too.

A rose trellis was built up against the side of the house and the corner of it barely butted up against the edge of the deck. I thought I might possibly be able to climb it, but I wasn't sure.

There might have been a ladder or something in the garage if I'd thought to look for one, but at the time I didn't. I was too tired to think of anything like that.

Instead I went to the rose trellis and started climbing. It was tricky, because the holes were just barely big enough for my shoes to fit inside, and some of them had big rose branches growing through them. The thorns tore holes in my jeans and stuck me in the hands and arms more than once on the way up, and that trellis was none too sturdy either. It swayed and creaked every time I made a move, making me think it was about to fall over any second. It's probably a thousand wonders it didn't.

I made it up there without falling, though, and then I had to grab hold of the edge of the deck and pull myself the rest of the way up. That was hard because I couldn't get any leverage with my feet except on that rickety trellis, so I had to pull up my whole weight with just my arms. As exhausted as I was right then, it took almost more strength than I had left.

I managed it finally, and left a big scrape on the side of my ribs when I dragged myself up over the splintery lip of the deck. It trickled a few little beads of blood. No worse than the thorn pricks on my hands and arms, but it stung.

I picked myself up and crossed the deck. There wasn't much up there except a wooden picnic table and a barbecue grill that somebody had made by cutting an oil barrel in half and putting hinges and handles on it. I thought that was pretty cool, actually, but it wasn't the time for idle curiosity.

I got up to the door and found it locked just like all the others. At least that's what I thought at first when I tried the knob and it wouldn't open. The knob turned, but when I pushed on the door it wouldn't move. I shoved harder, thinking maybe it was just stuck, but it was stubborn as a drunk mule no matter how hard I pushed.

I guess that shows how tired I was, because as soon as I tried pulling, the door opened without a hitch.

I stood there feeling really stupid for a minute or two, then I decided I better go on inside if I was going to. I was a little scared to go through with it, to tell the truth, but I didn't know what else to do at that point.

I buttered up my conscience by telling myself I wasn't going to steal anything or hurt anything, just sleep there for the night and then move on as soon as I could the next day. I still didn't like it, but if the place was for sale then at least I wouldn't be bothering anybody, I hoped.

I went inside and shut the door, which opened into a dark upstairs hallway. I tried the lights for a second just on the chance that they were still turned on, and I was surprised when they were. I turned them off again right away cause I didn't want anybody outside to see the light, but it was on long enough for me to see that there were three doors opening off the hall and some stairs leading down to other parts of the house.

I waited for a little while till my eyes adjusted to the dark, then I felt my way along the wall to the first door. It turned out to be a bathroom, and when I turned on the faucet I discovered the water was still running too.

I started to have a wild hope that I might actually get to take a shower, because goodness knows I needed one worse than I ever have in my whole life. But before I could get too excited I was disappointed to find out there was no hot water, just cold. I figured the water heater was probably turned off or something.

I went back out into the hall and continued with my exploring. Both of the other doors upstairs led into bedrooms, which was what I expected.

The first one looked like an old lady's room. There was enough moonlight coming through the window for me to make out a handmade quilt on the bed, and some powder boxes and perfume sprayers and pill bottles on top of the dresser, and some little whatnots of various kinds scattered here and there on shelves. It smelled like cinnamon potpourri, and it had that dusty, unused look of a room that nobody really lives in.

The other room looked like a guy's room, and it didn't have that empty unlived- in feel, either. It was darker in there because that side of the house faced away from the moon, but I could still see a little bit. There was a big bookshelf with a lot of paperback books on it. There were about six or seven baseball caps hung up on nails by the window, a computer on a desk, several pictures that I couldn't make out in the dim light, a rebel flag hung on the wall, some posters I couldn't read, and some other unidentifiable stuff.

I went downstairs and came out into a living room where there was a huge brown overstuffed couch and a big screen TV, and not really a whole lot else. The people didn't seem to believe in having a lot of furniture or knick-knacks, that's for sure.

The kitchen was blue and white tile, and there was a table in there in one corner. No dining room. I opened the refrigerator and found it stocked with food, even milk and eggs and stuff like that which doesn't keep too long. That made me a little bit uneasy cause it made me think maybe somebody lived there after all and it might not be a good idea for me to stay. I decided I couldn't worry about it right then, though. I just made up my mind to leave as soon as possible the next morning.

I did notice that the milk had been expired for almost a week, even though it didn't seem to have gone sour yet. I wondered if maybe the people had just not bothered to clean out the refrigerator when they left.

There were only two other rooms downstairs. One of them was for laundry and such, and the other one looked like a workshop. There was a countertop that ran all along one wall and a bunch of tools hung up above it and some pieces of equipment sitting here and there. I recognized a drill press and an air compressor with a hose coiled up beside it, but the other stuff it was too dark to see. I still didn't quite dare turn the lights on, not even down there.

There was a thermostat in the downstairs hallway and I did risk turning that light on, since it couldn't be seen from outside. The heat was turned down to 50 degrees, and that made me feel better about things. If anybody was staying there they would have had the heat turned up higher than that.

I turned it up to 70 and heard the furnace come on. I found the water heater in a closet in the hall and saw that it had been turned down real low too, so I turned it back up. There was a little wheel you had to turn, just like on the thermostat.

It didn't take long before the house was warm and cozy, and the water was running hot. That was just exactly what I wanted.

I stripped off my clothes and threw them in the washer and turned it on, then I went in the bathroom and had a long hot shower. I couldn't get enough of it. It felt so good I didn't get out till the water started to run cool again and my fingers were all wrinkled up. It was wonderful to be really clean again, especially after almost three weeks of barely washing at all. I even washed between my toes and inside my ears.

I didn't get out till there wasn't a drop of hot water left. I dried off and hung up my towel so it would dry, then stood and looked at myself in the mirror for a minute. I was pretty sure I looked a little thinner than I used to be, but other than that I didn't seem much the worse for wear. Same old sand-colored hair, same old bright blue eyes, same old snub nose with the pale little freckles scattered across it. You couldn't really even see them unless you looked close, but I knew they were there. I flexed my muscles a few times and pretended I was the Incredible

Hulk, and made a horrible face at myself. Mirrors always make me laugh.

I finally got tired of being silly and put on my last pair of boxer shorts. I didn't have anything else to wear because all my clothes were still wet in the washer. It was done washing by the time I came out of the bathroom, but I still had to put them in the dryer, and I wasn't going to wait an hour for them to get dry. I was so tired I could barely keep my eyes open. That hike from Commerce had just about killed me.

I went back upstairs to the guy's bedroom and fell onto the bed. It seemed like a better choice than the old lady's room, if only because I don't particularly like the smell of cinnamon. He also had a softer bed than she did. It felt like it was made out of one huge marshmallow under the sheets, just the way I like it.

I curled up under the comforter and I think I was asleep almost as soon as my head touched the pillow. I don't think I've ever slept so sweet in my life as I did that night.

When I woke up in the morning I could tell it was late. There was light shining in my face from the sun, and I moved my hand in front of my eyes to block it. I felt pretty good. I moved my legs and I could tell they were still a little stiff, but not too bad. Nothing like yesterday.

I stretched and yawned real deep, feeling soreness in every muscle, then I got up and padded down to the dryer in my bare feet to get my clothes. They were dry, so I put on some jeans and the *Poison* t-shirt, not bothering with socks and shoes right then. I folded the rest of the clothes and set them on top of the dryer so I could come back and stuff them in my pack before I left. They all fit in there pretty well now since I wasn't carrying all that bulky food around like I was when I left Tennessee.

I wanted to wash my jacket and my sleeping bag too, and so I threw those in the washer together and started it up. I decided I could wait that much longer before I left the house. Neither one of them would take long to drip dry.

After that I wandered into the kitchen to see if there was anything I wanted to eat. I felt bad about using all this stuff without asking, but what else could I do?

I drank some of the expired milk (which was still okay), and had a bowl of cereal. It was the cheap generic froot loops that come in a huge plastic bag from Wal-Mart, but that was okay. I didn't care about that cause they taste just the same anyway. I know, cause Jonathan's mom used to buy that kind and then use them to refill her empty box of real Froot Loops so everybody would think she bought the expensive kind. She was weird like that sometimes, like anybody would go snooping through the kitchen to see what kind of cereal she bought anyway. I smiled a little, remembering that.

I finished my breakfast and washed my bowl and spoon and glass and put them on the dish drainer to dry. Then I went back upstairs to get my shoes and make the bed while I was waiting on the washer to finish doing its thing. The least I could do for the guy whose house I'd slept in was to make sure I left it the way I found it.

It didn't take long to shoe my feet or finish the bed, and then I was left with nothing in particular to do for a while. I satisfied my curiosity by looking around in the guy's room a little more. I was too tired and I hadn't been able to see much last night.

Maybe I shouldn't have been so nosy, but I just think people are interesting, you know. I like to know what they're like and what they think about, deep down. People are all so different, and you can learn a lot about somebody from the things he puts in his room. This dude was no exception, and after a while I decided I liked him, whoever he was.

There were a couple of posters with Bible verses on them. One was about thinking about true and noble things, and the other one was about not giving up when things were hard. I could definitely relate to that one.

His baseball cap collection was interesting too. There was one from Texas A&M, and a camouflage one, and one from the Hard Rock Café in Dallas, and several others. I wondered if he really liked to play ball or if he was just a cap collector.

There was a picture of an old lady in a blue dress on the wall, and several pictures of a young woman with long brown hair. She was kinda pretty, except in one where she was sticking her tongue out at whoever was taking the picture.

It appealed to my curiosity, I guess, but by itself there was probably nothing in that room that I would have remembered a month later.

But that's when I hit the bombshell, and after that nothing was ever the same.

It was the last picture I looked at, way back on a corner of the bookshelf. I let my eyes fall on it carelessly, not expecting anything, and in a split second I recognized my mother.

She was a lot younger in that picture, but there was no mistaking it. She was standing next to Justin with a pine tree in the background, with the old lady in the blue dress from the other picture sitting down on a stool in front of them. It was the right house after all, and I'd found Justin at last.

Chapter Nine

I stood there open-mouthed for a minute. Here I'd been thinking I might still have to search half of Texas and maybe even then not find the man, and come to find out I'd been sleeping in his bed all night long and eating his food and didn't even know it. I had to have time to switch a few gears in my mind, let me tell you.

As soon as I could wrap my head around the idea that I'd actually found him, I was carried away by a flood of curiosity.

If this was Justin's house, then where was he at? Why was he selling it? Who was the old lady in the picture? Who was that girl with the long brown hair? Why was the phone disconnected? I had a thousand questions in my mind and no quick answers for any of them.

I satisfied my itch to understand by rooting through his desk drawers and his closet and anywhere else I could think of that might tell me something about him. I found a lot of interesting stuff.

I came across a couple of dried smelling oranges in his sock drawer, which reminded me of Mama. She always went out in the pasture and picked a couple of them to put in *my* sock drawer at home every fall. To make the clothes smell nice, she said. These were still fresh, not all dried out like they always got after a few weeks. I picked one up and smelled of it. It had that same sweet orangey smell I remembered, and for a second I was more homesick than I'd ever been since I left Tennessee. After a minute I put it back amongst the socks and moved on.

Justin didn't seem to wear much of anything except jeans and t-shirts, so that really didn't tell me much. He kept everything folded up neatly, and most of the shirts were nothing special. There was one that had Garth Brooks on it and another one with a picture of a lion roaring and holding some keys in its paw, and a caption that said *"The Lion of the Tribe of Judah has Triumphed!"*

I had better luck in his desk drawers. In the top drawer I found an old pay stub from an oil company in Atlanta, Texas, a place which I had never heard of before. I also found an old rent receipt for an apartment in Texarkana, Texas.

There was an AT&T cell phone bill addressed to Justin Wilder at this address. I opened it up and saw tons and tons of calls to Magnolia, Arkansas, but nothing else that really jumped out at me. I wondered who it was he called so much in that town.

In the other drawers I found a half empty box of orange Tic Tacs, a lot of miscellaneous papers and junk, some more photos of people I didn't recognize, a checkbook from Century Bank, and an expired Texas driver's license for Justin.

I picked up the driver's license and studied it for a while. Mama always used to complain that driver's license pictures look like mug shots, and I guess maybe they do. This one sure did. Justin looked about like he did in the picture I already had of him, except he was a little older and he wasn't smiling and looked like he was stoned. That made me feel better about recognizing him when we met.

I tried turning on his computer, but it was password protected and so I couldn't find out anything. There were limits to how snoopy I was willing to be, and trying to hack Justin's computer was way beyond the pale.

I found a .22 hunting rifle and some shells in the closet, and that pleased me. I can shoot pretty good when I want to. Daddy kept telling me I could have a real gun when I turned thirteen, but in the meantime I went shooting with Jonathan and his dad lots of times. There's an old rock quarry way back in the woods behind our house where we used to go set coke cans on top of boulders and either knock them off with the .22 or else blow them to kingdom come with the shotgun. I hardly ever missed.

You want to know something really weird, though? There was a whole separate box of .22 shells in that closet where the nose of the bullet was made of silver. I recognized it because the tip of the bullet was black instead of gray or coppery like it should have been, and when I rubbed the tarnish off then it got all shiny and bright.

I couldn't imagine where Justin had got such a thing, cause you can't exactly walk into a gun shop and ask for silver bullets. Not unless you want them to laugh at you. He must have special ordered them from somewhere. That made me very curious indeed about why he thought he needed something like that. The only thing silver bullets were good for that I knew of was to poison a *loup-garou* or make one very sick.

While I was rummaging through the closet, I noticed an access panel in the ceiling for getting into the attic. I thought about it a minute, then dragged the bedside table up to the closet door and climbed up there. It was none too sturdy, but the panel slid back easy enough and I was just tall enough to poke my head through into the attic.

It was dark and musty up there, and there wasn't much to see. Just a bunch of wires and insulation and stuff like that. No floor, and not even enough room to stand up straight if you climbed up there and stood on the rafters. It wasn't much more than a crawl space.

I was disappointed and about to go back down when I spotted an old Prince Albert cigar box half buried under some of the insulation. It was close enough to the access panel for me to grab it without getting up into the attic, so I pulled it out. I had to strain a little to reach that far, and just as I got hold of it the darned table fell over.

I hit the floor, of course, and smacked my shin on the door jamb so hard I felt sick at my stomach, but at least I didn't break anything. It just felt like I did.

I dropped the box when I fell, and it came open in midair and spilled out a bunch of change and dollar bills all over me and the floor.

As soon as my leg stopped hurting enough for me to think about anything else, I picked up the money and counted it on the bed. There was four hundred and sixty-three dollars and fifty-two cents. It was more money than I'd ever seen in my entire life. I guess Justin kept a slush fund at home in case the bank was closed or something like that.

I put the change back in the box and set it down on the desk in front of the computer. There was four hundred and fifty dollars in paper money, so I laid down on the bed and folded it up and turned it over and over in my hands for a little while. I knew I couldn't spend it because it wasn't mine, and I wasn't thinking about stealing it. I just liked the feel of holding that much cash in my hands. What can I say?

It made me wonder again where Justin had got off to. I could understand moving somewhere else and selling the house, but if that's where he was then I couldn't figure out why all his stuff was still here and the lights were still on. He couldn't be gone for good just yet. He'd have to come back here at some point to get his stuff, wouldn't he? And surely he wouldn't leave all that money in the attic and the food in the kitchen. I wouldn't have, if it was me.

The more I thought about it, the more certain I was that he'd come waltzing in sooner or later if I just waited long enough, and therefore the best thing I could possibly do right then was to stay exactly where I was for a while. If I stayed at the house then I'd have plenty of food and a warm place to sleep at night and everything else I needed, plus I'd be sure I wouldn't miss him if he showed up. If he came in and found me asleep in his bed or something then it might be sorta awkward trying to explain who I was and why I was there, but that was a problem I'd just have to deal with whenever it came. I hoped he wouldn't be too mad at me. But in the meantime there was no place else I could think of to go except back to Sulphur Springs, and that wasn't very practical at all.

So that's what I did. I spent my time doing various things. I laid on the overstuffed couch and ate popcorn and watched horror movies on the bigscreen, which were two things I was never allowed to do at home. Mama said she didn't like it when popcorn got in the carpet, and since Lola couldn't watch scary movies that meant I wasn't allowed to watch them either.

Justin had a big collection of movies to pick from; everything from *Nightmare on Elm Street* to *Scary Movie*, and when I got tired of horror flicks there was *Indiana Jones* and *The Day After Tomorrow* and even *The Lion King*.

There was also an Xbox and I thought at first that would be fun, but it didn't take long for me to find out he didn't have many games for it, and no cool ones at all. Just tennis and golf and boring junk like that, so I think I only played it maybe once or twice. It was mostly all movies when I was downstairs.

When I got tired of watching those I read some of his books. He had a lot of really old science fiction stuff and that was okay, but you get burnt out on anything after a long enough time. I'm a fast reader, and I sliced through *King Solomon's Mines* and *Perelandra* and *Journey to the Center of the Earth* in just three days. That's speedy even for me, but when you don't have much else to do then you can go pretty fast.

After about three or four days of sitting around the house I started to get a horrible case of cabin fever. It didn't even really help to go outside in the back yard, because there was nothing to do out there either. There was a bicycle and a four-wheeler outside, but both of them were locked up.

I thought about The Beast when I saw that bicycle and wished I had it with me. Ugly as it was, and no longer than I had it, I really liked that bike. I wondered if it was still under the trash at the burnt house and if Justin would maybe take me to Sulphur Springs to get it. I could polish it up, make it look a little nicer one of these days. If I'd had The Beast with me then at least I could have run around

Wolfe City a little bit and got out of the house now and then.

But on the other hand, maybe it was better I couldn't. I didn't want anybody to see me coming and going from the house, and I had to be there when Justin got back.

I did find a fishing pole and a tackle box in the garage, and a little exploring led me to a pond out in the woods behind the house. It wasn't a real big one as ponds go, but it looked like it might have some sweet bluegills in there. It had a thicket of bamboo growing on the far side which somebody had to have planted there. It was too tall and thick to be the wild kind. There were a few sweet gum trees on the bank, and the water was dark as iced tea from the leaves on the bottom.

That was on Friday afternoon when I discovered the pond, and since I had nothing particularly better to do I took the pole and the tackle box from the garage and sat down under a big magnolia tree that grew on the bank and fished for a while.

It was one of those warm days you get in December now and then, with lots of sunshine and just a little breeze, when it feels more like spring than winter, except you know it won't last. I was more or less recovered from my trip and back to my old self again. I'd been at the house since Tuesday night.

I wished Justin would hurry up and get home, but then again I didn't. I still didn't know what he'd say or if he'd even let me stay with him. I hadn't even nibbled on the question of what I'd do if he said no. But on the other hand, I really thought he was a person I could get along with, and I liked his place.

I guess I had this notion that he'd understand everything perfectly and not say a word about it, and he'd give me the extra bedroom for my own and we'd just live happily ever after. It was a nice thought, wasn't it?

One of my worst habits is that my imagination is too good. I build up all these wonderful daydreams about what I want and the best way things should go, and then it never ends up happening like that.

I started wondering what it would be like to go to school in Wolfe City and if they had a good baseball team. I wondered if Justin would take me to the lake during the summer and if I could have a horse someday like I'd always wanted, and if I'd make friends with any other kids.

I was so lost in daydreaming and painting myself this beautiful picture in my head that I didn't even notice when a man came walking up behind me through the woods. The path was clear of dead leaves, and he didn't make much noise in his tennis shoes.

He must have stood there and watched me for a while without me knowing, but finally he cleared his throat. I was so startled I dropped the fishing pole and whipped around to stare at him with bug eyes.

There was my Uncle Justin, no doubt about it, and he was looking at me with a frown on his face. Not quite a scowl, but he sure didn't look pleased to see me.

"Young feller, I don't mind you fishing in my pond, but I do expect you to ask me first. Specially when you borrow my pole and my tackle box too," he said. He had a thick Texas drawl, just like Mama does.

This was not the way I had hoped to run into Justin for the first time, with him thinking I was a sticky-fingered trespasser who took things without asking. It wasn't the best way to get things off on a good foot, not by any stretch of the imagination.

I took a deep breath and looked him right in the eye, like Daddy always told me I should do when talking to a grown man.

"Uh, you probably don't recognize me, but my name is Zach, and I think you're my Uncle Justin. I've been waiting to see you for a long time," I told him. I decided it was best to get right to the point.

His eyes narrowed a little bit and he stared at me long and hard. He looked like he didn't quite believe me.

"And what would make you think that, young feller?" he finally asked.

"Cause I know you have a sister named Jenna in Tennessee, and I'm her son. She gave me this," I said.

I fumbled in my pocket for that old picture of Justin I took from Mama's photo album, and offered it to him. He took it without thinking, and I could tell he recognized it. He looked back at me again, and this time his face was impossible to read. He still didn't look pleased, but I couldn't have told you what he was thinking to save my life.

"Where's Jenna then? Why are y'all here?" he demanded. He was starting to scowl for real now, and I knew I better say something quick.

"Mama is still back home. She's not with me. Nobody is with me. I came here alone cause I ran away before they could turn me into a monster cause I don't want to be one and you're the only person I knew who might help me," I blurted out all in one breath.

Justin looked thunderstruck when he heard that, but gradually I watched his expression soften up a little bit after he had a chance to take it all in.

"That's an awful long way, kid," he told me.

I thought about how long it had really been, and how lonely and hard and how I like to have never made it at all. Justin had no idea what an awful long way it had been.

I just nodded without saying anything.

Justin took his cap off and scratched his head and took a deep breath. I'm sure he was baffled and that me showing up was the last thing on earth he ever expected, but he handled it better than a lot of guys would have.

"Nobody knows you're here?" he asked me.

"No sir, nobody," I told him. He shook his head like he still couldn't quite believe it.

"I guess you better come up to the house and we best have a long, serious talk, boy," he finally said.

I wasn't sure if that sounded good or bad, but I was in no position to argue with him about it. All I could do was hope and pray he'd listen and see things my way. I did owe him an explanation, because I knew I was asking him for an awful big favor when he didn't even know me.

Justin turned around and walked up the path toward the house without looking back to see if I was following him. Maybe he hoped I wasn't, for all I knew. Most people are not too happy when you drop a big fat problem in their laps with no warning, and he was probably no exception.

He walked fast, and I had to trot to keep up with him. I left the fishing pole and the tackle box down by the pond cause I didn't want to remind him of me borrowing them without asking. Things were likely to be difficult enough already.

We came up into the back yard and I saw Justin's truck parked in front of the garage. He drove a black Dodge Ram

4x4, which was exactly the kind of truck I always wanted myself someday. He won a few extra points for that.

We came to the front door and he fished out his keys and unlocked it. He threw them carelessly in a basket just inside the foyer and then sat down at the kitchen table. He leaned back in his chair and waved me over to sit down myself, and when I did he just stared at me again until I thought he'd burn holes in me with his eyeballs.

"So talk," he finally told me.

Chapter Ten

So talk I did, for what seemed like a year. Justin listened without saying much, except to ask me a question or prod me to go on when I stopped for breath. He didn't grill me or act like he didn't believe me; he just sat there real quiet and took it in. It was hard to tell what he thought about it all.

I told him about the Ceremony and how I was supposed to kill something on the night of the next full moon to finish becoming a *loup-garou*. I told him why I didn't want to be one, and how Mama and Daddy meant to make me do it anyway whether I liked it or not. I told him about riding on the septic tank truck and the lady who bought my bus ticket in Fort Smith, and I told him how I found him on the Internet and how I lived in the dog house in Sulphur Springs and raked yards. I finally told him how I walked to his house from Cumby and got there Tuesday night. I didn't hide the fact that I'd been staying there waiting for him to come home, either. I figured if I wanted to live with the man, I better not start things off by lying to him.

Finally I wrapped it up, maybe an hour or so after we first came inside, and Justin put his face in his hands and didn't ask me anything else.

"Aw, man," he finally said, mostly to himself. That was all he said for a long time, but he finally looked at me.

"Well I'm not gonna turn you out on the street, Zach. But what do you want me to do? You know your mama's gonna come lookin' for you, don't you?" he said.

Now if I had to be totally honest, I'd have to admit I hadn't really thought that far ahead. Finding Justin and convincing him to let me stay with him was as far as I'd ever planned. When he pointed it out to me, I saw he was probably right. But whether he was or not, I couldn't let it go at that.

"I don't know what she might do. But I can't go back there, Justin, I just can't. You know what will happen to me if I do," I pleaded. He didn't look happy.

"Yeah, I know," he said, looking down at the table. There didn't seem to be anything else to say, and the silence dragged out till it started to get uncomfortable. At least it did for me; I guess Justin was too wrapped up in his own thoughts to notice.

"Your mama and me used to be pretty close, you know," he commented after a long time.

It didn't exactly have much to do with anything I had just told him, and I wondered why he said it. I have a bad habit sometimes of talking too much, but that night I managed to zip my lips and let Justin talk. It sounded like he might tell me some things I had wanted to know for a long time, if I had the sense to shut up and be quiet.

"We talked about everything, always did stuff together. Then she met your dad and got off into all that business he was in. You know what I mean," he said. I nodded without saying anything. I knew exactly what he meant.

"She was different then. Wasn't interested in anything else anymore. Wouldn't go to church, wouldn't do anything with her old friends anymore. She told me all about what was goin' on, let me watch her tear the throat out of a deer the next full moon. She wanted me to join up and do it with them too, even though I wasn't much older than you back then. She told me it was the most awesome feeling she ever had and I'd never be sorry I did it. But I never would go along. Didn't think it was right, and I told her so. Made her mad at me after awhile. We fought about it all the time. She started fighting with Paw and Gran, too, wouldn't listen to anything they told her anymore. They thought she was on drugs. I almost wish she had been," he said.

All this was news to me, but I resisted the urge to ask questions. I kept quiet as a mouse.

"Finally she and your dad pulled up stakes and said they was gettin' married and movin' away. They never said where. After that I never heard hide nor hair else till you showed up on my pond today," he told me. He sounded sad.

"You never tried to find her?" I ventured to ask.

"No, she made it clear she was done with me and all the rest of us. Like to have killed Paw and Gran, cause they raised us both you know. Paw never did get over it. I think he died partly from grief, a couple years after Jenna went off and disappeared. I lived here with Gran till she passed away this past summer, except when I was workin' in the oil fields. She woulda been proud to meet you, Zach. I wish she could have," he went on.

I wasn't sure what to say to that either.

"I'm sorry," I finally told him.

"Aw, you couldn't help it, bubba. Don't worry about it. But we have to think what to do with you, though. I'm not set up too good right now for takin' care of a kid. I'm gone all week, and I was fixin' to sell this place and move closer to work. You'd have to be in school and all that, and sooner or later they'd find you if they looked. I'm not that hard to find," he told me.

I had my own opinion about how hard Justin was to find, but I didn't think it was a good time to mention that.

"They don't know I was lookin' for you, and I never said anything to them," I pointed out. He still looked doubtful, and I was desperate to change his mind. I knew if I couldn't convince him now, I'd never be able to do it later.

"You could go ahead and sell this place and we could move to wherever your work is. I don't mind that. And I'm old enough to take care of myself," I promised.

"What about school, though?" he asked.

"I don't know, I could tell them I was in home school or something up till now. They wouldn't know any better. You could tell them I'm your nephew who just came to live with you. People do that kind of stuff all the time. I'm sure it would be okay," I said.

I tried to sound as confident and sure of myself as I possibly could, cause I knew if I sounded like I had any doubts, then Justin would end up having at least ten times as many. He thought about it for what seemed like a long time, and then he took a deep breath, like he'd made up his mind.

"Well, we've still got a little while before it matters much. You can probably miss this last week or so before Christmas, and then you won't have to be back in school until after New Year's. Maybe we can figure somethin' out by then," he finally said.

"So I can stay?" I asked him hopefully, hardly daring to believe it. He finally smiled then, for the first time since I met him.

"Yeah, Zach, you can stay," he told me. A surge of relief washed over me and I didn't mind at all letting him see how happy I was to hear that. I jumped up and threw my arms around the dude and gave him a bear hug.

"Whoa, bubba, slow down," he laughed, "We still got a lot of things to figure out."

I knew that was true, but right then I didn't care. I was too happy to have a home again after all that time.

We talked for a long time that day, about a bunch of different things. I really liked him a lot. He was funny and pretty smart too. He was a geobiologist for an oil company, whatever that was. I never did quite understand what it was he did. I just knew he had to travel a lot to drilling sites and that kept him away from home except on the weekends, mostly. That was why he'd been gone all week.

After a while, the winter daylight started fading away and Justin noticed it.

"Come on, boy, if you're gonna stay with me awhile then you need some stuff. You can't go around in holey shirts and wore-out jeans," he told me, getting up from the table and heading for the door. I got up and followed him.

We went outside and jumped in his truck, and he drove to the Wal-Mart in Commerce. I remembered walking that road just four days ago, and it's amazing how much faster you can get somewhere when you drive, isn't it?

We went inside and he bought me some new clothes and a toothbrush and a Texas Rangers baseball cap and some new tennis shoes. He got me a prepaid cell phone so I could call him if I needed to, and he gave me thirty bucks to spend however I wanted.

It had been quite a while since I had that much spending money for whatever I wanted. I bought myself a George Strait CD and saved the rest for later. You never knew when you might need some extra cash. I'd learned that lesson real well.

After that, he took me down the street to the Lone Star Pizza Works by the football stadium. We ordered an extra large sausage and pepperoni pizza with double cheese, which is my favorite. When the food got there, he asked a blessing before we ate. I'd seen people do that before, of course, but not in quite a while.

Justin smiled and laughed a lot and seemed like he'd changed his mind and decided to be glad I was around. He made me feel like he was glad, anyway, and that was something I wasn't used to and hadn't expected. I would have been satisfied if he'd just agreed to let me stay with him. He didn't have to do all this extra stuff he was doing, and I loved him for it.

There are times when I look back and think how strange it was that he won me over so fast like that. Maybe it had something to do with me being alone and far from home, but it wasn't only that. I didn't know what it was about him that I loved so much, not back then, but I do now. It was goodness. He walked close with God and he really lived it. You don't find too many like that. It took me a long time to learn what it was that made him so different, cause until I met Justin I never saw it before. At the time, I just knew he was the best uncle I ever had.

Well, he was the only uncle I ever had, to be honest, but you know what I mean. Mama didn't have any other brothers or sisters, as far as I knew, and I didn't know anything at all about Daddy's family, except Nana Maralyn. Like I said before, nobody in my family ever talked about their relatives if they weren't monsters. I thought Daddy was an only child, but I wasn't totally sure.

"Yeah, your dad was from Sulphur Springs, just down the road a piece. That's really all I know about him. Only met him a couple times. He never mentioned any family except his mama, and you already knew about her," Justin told me when I asked him, shrugging his shoulders.

That wasn't really a whole lot more than I already knew, but I decided it wasn't so important to know right now. I could always find out more later.

After we finished our pizza, Justin took me to a movie rental place and got some games for the Xbox, and then we drove back home. He played some games with me and beat me at baseball, but that was no surprise. He'd had a lot more time to play the game than I had. If it had been a real baseball game outside then I would have beat the tar out of him. I'm the best pitcher on my team.

But he beat me fair and square on the Xbox, so I tackled him and knocked him down on the floor and we rolled around and wrestled until he pinned me down by the couch and I had to give up.

I hadn't done anything like that in years. Daddy used to wrestle with me when I was little, but not in a long time. Maybe it was because Justin was younger and still enjoyed stuff like that, or maybe he just liked me better. I don't think it's wrong to say that, cause you can love somebody without really liking them very much. You have to have something in common to be able to like a person.

I think maybe me and my dad had that problem, cause we didn't care about the same things. So I guess he probably maybe loved me, but he didn't much like me as a person. You can always tell.

It was different with Justin though. He laughed at stuff I thought was funny, and talked about things I thought were interesting, and enjoyed stuff I liked myself. He was so much like me. I'd only met him half a day ago, and I could tell that already.

There are times when God gives you things that are so good you never would have dared to ask for them or even dream they were possible. Justin was like that. I don't think I ever told him so, but I hope he knows it.

We spent that whole weekend at the house, mostly, just talking and doing things, and we drove around Wolfe City a little bit. I got to see where he and Mama went to high school and I got to visit the cemetery where my grandparents were buried. They died in a car wreck when Justin was only a baby, so he and Mama had to live with *their* grandparents till they grew up.

I learned lots of things like that which I never knew before. I filed it all away in my mind to think about later, when there was more time.

Every night Justin called his girlfriend Eileen in Magnolia and they talked for at least an hour or two. She was the girl in the pictures with the long brown hair who liked to stick out her tongue at him. He told her about me and some of the reasons why I was there, and it didn't seem to faze her any. I talked to her for a minute myself just cause she wanted to say hi to me. She sounded like a nice person, the best I could tell.

Sunday morning Justin took me to church with him, and I was afraid I wouldn't like that at first. I almost said I didn't want to go. But I didn't want to disappoint him, so I bit my tongue and went. I expected it to be dull and boring, but it really wasn't. When we got there he sent me to the youth group and said he'd pick me up later.

I had more fun than I thought I would. They had a band and we mostly sang songs that were easy to learn. Then we studied something from the Bible, but I have to confess I don't remember what it was. Something about Christmas, no doubt, but I forget exactly what. We played some games and finally we had a potluck dinner of chicken spaghetti and garlic bread with grape Kool-Aid and peanut butter cookies. I decided if church was like that every Sunday then I might not mind going after all.

Going to church wasn't the only thing I had to get used to, living with Justin. People always have their own personal habits and ways of doing things, and he was no exception. He ate whole wheat bread and he liked to crunch ice cubes with his teeth while he watched movies and he had a bad habit of liking to get up at the crack of dawn every day.

That one was especially hard for me to get used to, because when he got up the first thing he always did was go in the bathroom and shave.

That by itself might have been okay, except he always sang while he did it, and that woke me up every time. He also sang in the shower, and in the truck, and sometimes just around the house while he worked on things. He was just happy I guess, but it wasn't something I had ever seen somebody do so much. He sang anything from country love songs to old hymns to *Camptown Races* and *Oh Susannah.* You just never could tell what might pop into his head. There were times when I wanted to laugh at him for it, and late Sunday afternoon I finally did, when he was singing *Grandma Got Run Over By a Reindeer* at the top of his lungs. I swear I couldn't help it, I just busted out laughing.

He stopped singing and gave me an innocent look.

"What is it?" he asked, like he didn't already know.

"Aw, just you singin' all the time," I finally managed to gasp."

"What, you don't like my singin'?" he asked, pretending he was all hurt and brokenhearted.

"Yeah, you're just silly cause you do it all the time, that's all," I told him. He didn't seem the least bit perturbed by that, and he ruffled my hair and jumped onto the couch.

"Come here, bubba, we need to talk about some things," he told me. He was taking up most of the couch himself because he was lying down sprawled out like a warm breakfast, but I sat on the end of it by his feet. He sat up to give me more room.

"You know I have to go to work tomorrow, right?" he told me.

"Yeah, I know that. I'll be okay," I said. I wasn't really looking forward to another week at the house by myself, but I was okay with it. I'd find something to amuse myself.

"Well, I been thinkin' about that, Zach, and I don't think it's such a good idea for you to stay here all week by yourself," he said.

"Where else would I go?" I asked, not really liking the way the conversation was going. I guess deep down I was afraid he'd changed his mind and decided I couldn't stay with him anymore. Was this just a long winded way of breaking the bad news to me gently?

As it turned out I was worrying for nothing. He wasn't thinking anything like that at all.

"I think I'll take you to work with me this week, and maybe that way you can help me look for a new place. You kinda caught me by surprise, Zach. I was gonna move, but not this soon. Now we have to move things up a little bit," he said, rubbing his stubbly goatee.

I didn't know much of anything about Texas or where he needed to work or anything like that, so I didn't think I had much advice to give. I didn't feel like I had a right to demand anything from him, anyway.

"Aw, I'd be happy with anything you could find, Justin," I told him.

"Yeah, I'm sure you would, bubba, but all the same I'm sure there are things you like and things you don't," he said.

That was true, and since he was the one who asked I felt better about telling him some of what I really wished for.

"Well, can it be somewhere in the country, sorta like this?" I asked. He smiled again.

"Yeah, we can probably manage that part without too much trouble, Zach," he told me.

"What about somewhere with hills, and rivers to swim in, and a place where I can go horse riding?" I asked him, encouraged by the way he was so easygoing about it. I was mostly thinking about Tennessee when I said that, and I guess he knew it.

"We. . . ll, maybe," he said, "We'll have to see what we can find."

He didn't seem too sure about that part, so I left it at that. I was sure he'd do the best he could, and I knew I ought to be thankful for whatever I got. But I'd be lying if I said I didn't miss the mountains and the wild hickory trees, and the sound of whitewater falling over rocks. They say there's no place like home, and I guess that's true. I missed it more than I ever thought I would.

I let my mind drift away for a minute, thinking about all the things I'd left behind. The mountains and the whitewater, Jonathan, going target practicing in the quarry, my bike, my family, school. . . where should I even start? If I made a list of things, I could probably go on and on till the cows came home and still leave out a bunch. How could I ever even begin to replace it all?

The answer to that one was easy, of course. There wasn't any way. You can never have the same thing twice, and it's hopeless to try. It never works like that, and all you end up doing is breaking your heart against a solid rock. That's why when you lose things you have to let them go instead of trying to get them back again. You can't do it, and you only hurt yourself worse if you keep on. Never cry for the moon.

I'm not sure who told me that or where I learned it, but even back then I already knew it was the truth. The sooner I stopped thinking about the past and started focusing on making a new life for myself, the happier and better off I'd be.

Chapter Eleven

"So where do we stay this week, then?" I asked abruptly. It was mostly for the sake of changing the subject, so I wouldn't be thinking about home anymore.

"Texarkana. It's close to where I work most of the time," he said.

So we gathered up clothes and stuff for a week and piled in the truck. Justin locked up the house and headed down through Commerce and Cumby and got on the interstate and headed east.

"How long will it take to get to Texarkana?" I asked him not long after we left.

"Aw, just about two and a half hours," he said.

Justin is one of those people who doesn't like to talk much while he's driving, so I didn't try to make conversation with him anymore right then. I looked out the window at the woods and the cow pastures beside the freeway instead, and thought about how unreal it all seemed. The whole journey from Tennessee to Texas felt almost like it happened to somebody else, a long long time ago. I was glad it was over.

I did get one sharp reminder, though. When we went through Sulphur Springs, Justin stopped and got us something to eat at that Taco Bell by the interstate. I didn't tell him it was the same one where I used to go and eat bean burritos because it was all I could afford.

He wouldn't let anybody have food in his truck cause he said it made a mess. So we got out and ate inside the restaurant, and I didn't let on how much I didn't like the memories it brought back. Like I said, I'd just as soon forget about all that. But Justin didn't know, and I kept it to myself. There was no reason to bum him out over something he couldn't help.

There was one thing I wanted while I was in Sulphur Springs, though, if I could talk him into doing it.

"Hey Justin, can we do something real quick before we leave Sulphur Springs?" I asked him.

"Maybe so. We're not in that big of a hurry. What's on your mind, Zach?" he asked me.

"Well, if there was time and you didn't mind doing it, I just wanted to get my bike while we're here," I said.

"Is it far?" he asked.

"No, not too far. I can show you how to get there," I told him. Justin shrugged.

"Sure, if you want to, Zach. We'll have to lay down a blanket or something in the truck bed so it doesn't scratch the paint, though," he said.

That was fine with me, so after we left Taco Bell I showed him where to drive until we came to that weedy vacant lot where I had my second home. When I counted up the days,

I realized I'd only lived there for a little more than a week and a half, but it seemed like a whole lot longer than that in my memory.

We pushed our way through the vines and bushes until we got back there where the dog house was. It was just like I left it six days ago, with the little padlock still hung on the door.

"So this is where you stayed all that time, huh?" Justin asked me, looking at everything.

"Uh-huh," I told him. While we were there I decided to get the rest of my stuff, so I pulled out my key and unlocked the door.

It smelled like hay and wild cherries inside, and for a second I had a powerful memory of crawling in there to sleep at night. Justin stuck his head inside after me.

"I'm amazed you made all this yourself, Zach. You're a pretty smart cookie," he told me, looking at the door and the hay and the lamp and everything else.

It felt good to hear him say that. I hadn't been thinking anything except trying to stay alive when I was living there, but I was glad he thought I had done all right.

I gathered up my books and my oil lamp, and somehow the place seemed empty without them. I could have taken my padlock too, I guess, but for some reason I didn't. I just snapped it back on the hasp and locked the place up. It seemed like the right thing to do. I'd probably never come back there again, but it was *my* place, in its own unique way, and I didn't want to leave it in bad shape.

We dug The Beast out from under the burnt wood, and it seemed just as good as it always was, and just as ugly. Justin laughed when he saw it.

"You really want that old thing, Zach?" he asked me.

"Yeah, I really do," I told him. I couldn't have said *why* I wanted it, except maybe because it had a colorful story behind it now and that gave it some character. We'd been through a lot together, me and that bike, and I didn't want to leave it behind. Justin was laid back enough that he didn't much care, so we carried it out front to the road where the truck was parked. Then we laid my sleeping bag down over the truck bed and put The Beast on top of it.

"Need to get me a bed liner one of these days," Justin told me while we loaded the bike.

That was about all there was to it. We drove down past the Southwest Dairy Museum and the carwash where I used to get my water, and then got back on the interstate. Not long after that we left Sulphur Springs behind.

It took about two more hours to get to Texarkana, maybe a little less. I had been asleep when I came through there on the bus two weeks ago, so everything was all new to me.

Justin got off the interstate onto Summerhill Road and drove all the way downtown to Seventh Street. It didn't look like a very nice neighborhood, and when he pulled into a cheap-looking motel I wasn't surprised. That was the only kind I'd seen for a while. This one was painted-over brick, sorta old and run down, and it advertised weekly rates. Justin parked the truck in front of Number 3.

"Now this place ain't much, Zach. I just use it as a place to sleep and clean up while I'm workin', cause it's cheap and it's never been anybody but me. So don't expect too much," he warned me.

He didn't need to tell me that. I already didn't expect too much, just from looking at the outside of the place. I was good about keeping a poker face and not letting myself look disappointed, though. And I really wasn't, not all that much. After you've lived in a dog house for a few days then a run-down motel is a piece of cake. Justin went to the office and got a key, then let us inside.

The place was just as run down and old inside as it was out. The walls were painted a dark brown to hide dirt, almost the same color as the carpet. The carpet had cigarette burns on it, and so did the blanket on the bed. It smelled dank and musty and when we turned the lights on I swear I saw a roach run under the bed out of the corner of my eye.

I didn't say anything about it, but I was hoping we wouldn't have to stay there very long. Justin looked sheepish, and I knew he'd seen the roach too.

"Like I said, it's not much, but we only have to stay here till Thursday," he told me. Well, that answered that question at least.

We took our clothes and stuff out of the truck and put them in the room, and then we watched a movie on TV for a while. I think it was *Weird Science*, but I can't remember for sure. I wasn't paying much attention.

Eileen called at eight, and after that Justin was occupied talking to her for the rest of the evening.

I didn't mind. I watched the rest of the movie and then a couple more shows on TV and then I went to bed about eleven.

Justin woke me up the next morning while he was doing his shaving and singing thing, but I went right back to sleep before he walked out the door. It was still dark outside when he left.

I finally woke up about eight thirty, I guess. My bike was sitting in front of the TV, and Justin had left a key on the table by the door with a ten dollar bill and a note written on a page torn out of the back of the phone book.

Zach, there's several stores not far from here when you get hungry, but don't get lost. I'll be back about six. Call me if you need me.

I noticed he'd also left a business card with the name and address and phone number of the motel, just in case I did get lost I guess, and he'd put my phone on the charger before he left. He always thought about little things like that.

I took a shower and put on some clean clothes, and stuck the money and my phone and the room key and the business card in my pocket, and then I pushed The Beast outside and locked the door. I felt like it was high time for some breakfast.

I wasn't sure which way to go, since I didn't know where anything was. I headed west so the sun wouldn't be shining in my face; it seemed like as good a way to go as any. I was on a fairly major street, so as long as I didn't turn anywhere I probably wouldn't get lost.

It wasn't too cold that morning, but it was fairly cloudy and looked like it might rain later on. I rode The Beast for maybe ten or twelve blocks, and passed under a freeway overpass. I came to a McDonalds and had a sausage and cheese biscuit. I don't especially like McDonald's, but they'll do in a pinch.

If I'd known where anything was, I might have gone somewhere else and found something to do. But that first day I didn't, so I got a burger and a coke for later and then I rode back to the motel and stayed there the rest of the day till Justin got back.

There was nothing to do besides watch TV all day, and I was sick of that after just a few hours. My books were still in Justin's truck.

That turned into my regular schedule the rest of the time we spent at the motel, and let me tell you, four days can seem like a long time when you're bored. Justin got back to the motel about six o'clock every night and usually took me somewhere to eat and maybe to do something fun if he wasn't too tired. I knew sometimes he was a lot more worn out than he pretended to be, but he always tried to take care of me the best he could. He was a good man.

We ended up staying Thursday night too, cause Justin wanted to get up early and have the whole day to get stuff done, he said. There was no reason to go to Wolfe City on Thursday night just to turn around and come right back to Texarkana the very next day. I could see the logic in that, but that didn't mean I had to like it.

I endured it somehow, but I'll tell you, I've never been so glad to see the last of a place as I was that nasty motel. Me and roaches don't get along.

We got up early Friday morning and left the motel about seven or so. For once I didn't mind getting up early, because Justin said we needed to go looking for a house that day, among other things.

He stopped at an Exxon station and got a newspaper, then fished a blue pen out of the glove box and started reading the sale ads to see if there was anything that looked interesting. He also made some phone calls to several real estate agents and stopped by a couple of offices. He wouldn't let me go inside when he did that, so I don't know what he said or what happened. He usually came out with a few sheets of paper that had pictures of houses and information about them.

After that, we started driving around to look at places. Justin had worked there long enough that he was able to get around pretty much without a map most of the time.

Texarkana is sorta strange. Half of it is in Texas and the other half is in Arkansas, so I was never completely sure what state I was in. When we went past the post office downtown, he stopped and took a picture of me with one foot on each side of the border. I knew we didn't have a whole lot of time to dawdle, but he was never in such a hurry that he didn't have time for fun stuff like that. I still have that picture somewhere, I think.

The first house we looked at was on Buchanan Road, and it was okay I thought. It was a brick one with three acres of pine woods behind it. But Justin vetoed that one until we looked at all the others first. He said it was better to know what all your choices were before you made up your mind about something like that. I'm sure he was right.

We looked at a lot of houses that day; I don't remember exactly how many. At least ten or twelve. As laid back and easygoing as he usually was, I can honestly say I've never seen Justin as picky and demanding as he was with those houses. There always seemed to be something he didn't like about every one we saw. Some were too old, some were not big enough, and some didn't have enough land with them. There was always something missing. He was a lot more particular than I would have been. But he was the one spending the money, so I guess he had a right to be as choosy as he wanted to be.

Finally, when I had just about decided he'd never be satisfied with anything, we found a place he liked.

It was east of town, where there were some hills covered in woods. There was a place out there up on the side of a hill where you could look out over Coca Cola Lake. It came with ten acres, and a wooden dock down on the lake shore, and a fenced in pasture, and a bunch of oak and hickory trees all around.

The house itself was just one story, white, with a deep porch and four square columns across the front. It had three bedrooms, one for me, one for Justin, and one for extra space. There was a built-on shed for all of Justin's tools, and it was way out in the country with no close neighbors. It seemed like it had everything a boy could ever want, and I fell in love with it right away.

"I think this is the best place we saw all day," I told him after we had walked around and looked at it.

We were standing on the porch looking out across the lake when I said that. I've never been sure why they call it Coca Cola Lake, unless maybe it's because the water is sorta dark. But it didn't look dark that day. It looked blue as a marble that some really big giant kid had dropped in the valley.

"Yeah, I think maybe this is the one we want, Zach," Justin agreed.

He went to the real estate agent that very afternoon and shook hands on the deal. I never knew things could get done that fast. They just signed some papers, and the agent handed Justin the keys, and that was that.

"Well, Zach, we got a choice, you and me. We can go back to the motel for one more night, or we can stay at the house tonight instead. Which would you rather do?" he asked me when we got back outside. As if there was any doubt!

"I think we should definitely stay at the house tonight," I told him. If I never saw that nasty roach motel again in my life it would be way too soon.

So we went to the store and got an air mattress and some blankets and pillows and candles. There was no furniture in the house, and no water or electricity either, but neither one of us minded roughing it for one night. Justin called the power company and they said it would be Monday before they could come turn the electricity on. He didn't have to worry about water, because there was a well with an electric pump, so as soon as the power came on then the water would too.

We ordered a pizza and some boneless hot wings and went back to the house not long before it started getting dark. We lit the candles and I lit my oil lamp from Sulphur Springs, and we blew up the air mattress and laid it against the wall. Then we sat there crosslegged and ate our pizza and drank some coke.

It can be really quiet in a house at night when there's no electricity to run anything. There are none of those little background noises from the refrigerator humming or a heater running or anything like that. You never notice those things till they aren't there anymore.

"Tomorrow I guess we need to go back to Wolfe City and start loading things up. That may take awhile," Justin said.

"It didn't seem like there was a lot of stuff to me," I said.

"Not so much at the house, no. But a lot of stuff I already packed up in boxes and put in a storage building, Zach. We have to get all that, too," he told me. I hadn't known that before, but it made sense. I always did think the downstairs part of the house looked awfully sparse.

"It might be a bigger job than you think it will, but I hope we can get it all done over the weekend if we give it all we've got," he went on. I thought he was probably right.

There wasn't much to do with no electricity, so we went to bed not long after that, intending to get up early and head for Wolfe City.

I have to say, it was doggone cold in that house with no heat after the sun went down. It reminded me of that first night when I ran away from home and had to sleep inside the septic tank. It wasn't quite *that* bad, but cold enough. I slept next to Justin on the air mattress and we put all the blankets on top of us. It wasn't too bad like that, except his feet were like blocks of ice every time one of them touched me.

I couldn't go to sleep for a long time that night, partly from Justin's icicle toes and partly because it was so quiet and still. I'm used to at least a little bit of noise at night, and now all I could hear was Justin breathing.

He must have thought I was asleep though, because after a while he put his hand on top of my head and started talking real soft and low so I could barely hear him. I don't know what all he said, but I heard something about asking God to remember me and bless me. When he was done he smoothed my hair down and pulled his arm back under the covers, and before long he was asleep.

I never had anybody pray over me like that before, at least not that I know of. I wondered if he'd ever done it before when I really was asleep, and what he might have said. He could still surprise me sometimes with things like that, no matter how well I thought I knew him.

I hope I can be like that someday.

We spent that whole weekend going back to Wolfe City and renting a U-Haul and loading it up with all the stuff from the house and the storage building over there. Justin wasn't a pack rat, but it seems like there's always more to load up than you think there will be. It took three trips to move everything.

The old house looked empty and lonesome with all the stuff gone, and Justin seemed a little sad. I guess it's always hard to walk away from where you grew up and everything you remember after so many years. I know the feeling.

"Well, there it is," he said to himself when we loaded up the last two boxes. Before we left, he cut some branches from the rose bush on the trellis and put them in a Ziploc bag with a little water.

"Gran always loved these roses," he told me. They were red ones, with white and pink streaks in the middle. Later on, he planted them all along the front porch at the new house, and they took hold real well.

We finished moving everything by Sunday afternoon, and Justin didn't have to work the whole next week cause it was Christmas.

We spent all day Monday working our tails off getting stuff unloaded and put away in the right places. It seems like that took even longer than packing everything.

We didn't quite finish. The extra bedroom was still stacked full of cardboard boxes, but at least all the major big stuff was put where it belonged. Justin said we'd worry about the rest of it after Christmas.

Early the next morning, which was Christmas Eve, we took the truck out in the woods on a dirt road and chopped down a big cedar tree and set it up in the living room in a five gallon bucket filled with water and rocks. Most of the ornaments were still stashed in one of those boxes in the extra room, so that called for a trip to town to buy some more.

While we were out shopping for ornaments, Justin took me to a flea market and got me a bunk bed for my room. I was sorta surprised the place was still open on Christmas Eve, but on second thought maybe it's not that surprising. They were probably trying to sell as much as they could at the last minute.

While we were at the flea market I waited till Justin wasn't looking, and I spent ten bucks to get him a coffee mug with a wolf on it, full of butterscotch candy. That was his high school mascot in Wolfe City. The wolf, that is, not the butterscotch. I knew it wasn't much, and I knew I was buying it for him with his own money that he gave me, but it was something I really wanted to do. The old lady who ran the mug booth wrapped it up for me and put it in a bag before he got back. He never noticed I bought it.

We spent maybe another hour or two at the flea market after that, getting some other things we needed. I got all new stuff for my bedroom to finish it out; a bean bag chair and a wooden desk and some green blankets and a couple of posters and pennants and such. The only things I ended up having in there from Tennessee were my *Robinson Crusoe* book, my backpack, and the few clothes I brought with me. I got rid of those old ones from Sulphur Springs, but I kept my oil lamp and a couple of the books I got while I was there. Of course I still had The Beast too, but it was outside in the shed.

When it was finished it didn't look anything at all like my old room, but like I said before, that was probably a good thing. The less I was reminded of that, the better.

Chapter Twelve

After we got back from the flea market, Justin left me alone at the house for a couple of hours that afternoon while he went back into town. He still had some things he wanted to get, he said.

I tried to make myself useful while he was gone. I hung curtains and put away the silverware and things like that. I couldn't unpack many of the boxes because I wasn't sure where the stuff was supposed to go, but I did what I could.

After a while I went outside and wandered down by the lake to stand on the dock. You could tell it was old, but the wood was still solid. It ran out into the lake about thirty feet. The water was too dark and the day was too gray to tell how deep it was. There was no wind at all, and the surface was smooth as a big mirror, reflecting the bare gray limbs of the trees all along the bank.

It was peaceful, and I decided not to disturb it by throwing rocks in the water like I might usually have done.

The lake was small enough that you could see the other shore with no trouble. I guess there might have been houses and things all along the bank, hidden back behind the trees. You couldn't see them, though. For all I could tell, I might have been the only person in the world who ever laid eyes on the place.

I liked that idea. It made me feel like an explorer in some new and unknown land. The dock under my feet sorta spoiled that illusion, but as long as I didn't look down I could still pretend. Sometimes my imagination gets the better of me.

You could see a long way to the west, and I sat there for about an hour and watched the sun go down across the lake. I didn't say anything, didn't do anything, just watched. It was gold and crimson and orange, and it turned the water gold where the light touched.

I sat there until the sun slipped down below the edge of the world and everything started to turn gray. There was getting to be just a little bit of a chill in the air, so I got up and walked back home.

It's strange, but I think watching that sunset from the dock is when I first started thinking of that house as home. Always up till then when I thought of home I thought of my mom and dad's house in Tennessee, but after that, home was Justin's place.

Why then? I honestly couldn't tell you why, except that sometimes you just feel things. It's sort of like when you're waking up real slow in the morning and you finally know you're awake and not dreaming anymore. It had been growing down deep for a long time, and that was when it finally broke the surface. I wish I could put it into words better.

When Justin got back he had bunches of presents with him, some for me and some for Eileen. They were already wrapped so there was no chance of sneaking a peek at what they were. Not that I would have done that anyway, you know; I'm just saying nobody could have done it even if they *did* want to.

A little bit later Eileen came over. I heard her pull up in the yard, but she didn't come inside right away. Justin had me busy making popcorn, so I didn't think much about it at the time, even though I was really curious to meet her.

I knew a little bit about her already. I knew she was a chemist for the same oil company where Justin worked, and they had to share lab space. I guess that's probably how they first met, talking about oil and grease and all that other funky stuff they have to work with all the time.

But whatever it was they used to talk about, I knew here lately they'd been talking a lot about me. So Justin told me, and that made me even more curious about her than I would have been otherwise.

Eventually she did come in, carrying several more packages in her arms. I was disappointed to see that hers were already wrapped too. She was too much like Justin that way; she never missed a lick.

"So here's the amazing Zach," she said when she walked in, smiling at me.

It was the first time I'd ever seen her in person, and I have to admit she was prettier in real life than she was in those pictures. Maybe it's because she didn't stick her tongue out at me, but I think it's because she was just really beautiful.

She set her packages down and kissed me on the cheek and said she was sure we'd get along just fine. I don't even remember what I told her cause she made me turn red, but I liked her an awful lot.

Sometimes I wonder why Eileen kissing me made me turn red, when that lady who kissed me in the bus station in Fort Smith didn't do that? A kiss is a kiss, isn't it? Justin saw my face and thought it was hilarious, but then of course he *would* think it was funny.

"Looks like you two are gonna be really good friends," he said, still laughing at me a little.

"Uh, yeah," I said, or something like that. I was still a little tongue-tied.

He finally contained himself and let me off the hook by suggesting that we sing some Christmas carols.

Justin wanting to sing was nothing unusual, so that's what we did. He and Eileen did, anyway. I didn't really know all the words; I just sang the parts I remembered. They took turns picking the songs. I remember he wanted to sing *Oh Come All Ye Faithful* and she wanted to sing *Silent Night*, and there were some others I didn't recognize. They wanted me to pick one too, but when I said I couldn't think of anything they didn't insist. After we got done singing then we opened all the presents.

That was something else a little unusual about Justin that I wasn't used to, that he opened gifts on Christmas Eve night instead of Christmas morning. He said it was because it was more like when the wise men came to bring their gifts to Jesus, and that's what Christmas was supposed to be about, not Santa Claus. I guess that's true, but I never heard anybody say that before.

Justin and Eileen gave each other lots of things, I don't remember what all. I remember she gave him a red and white Santa cap and he was silly enough to wear it all night. He gave her some diamond earrings and a pair of leather gloves, among other things.

Justin smiled when he opened the mug I gave him and passed out some of the butterscotch to everybody. He said it was perfect to go on his desk at work. As far as I know that's where he still keeps it, to hold pencils and things.

Besides the kiss, Eileen gave me a pair of cowboy boots and a couple of games for the Xbox. Justin gave me some money and some more clothes, and a remote control monster truck. But then, he'd been buying me stuff all week too.

They both saved the best thing for last, though.

After everything was opened and the wrapping paper was piled up in snowdrifts all over the floor, I thought that was all of it. But then Justin stood up, looking all mysterious.

"I think maybe we forgot somethin', didn't we, babe?" he asked Eileen.

"Yeah, I think maybe we did," she told him, smiling. They both looked at me.

"What is it?" I asked, cause I really didn't have a clue what they were talking about.

"Go outside and see," Eileen told me. I was game, so I got up and put on my jacket and went outside.

Tied up to a tree in the front yard next to Eileen's truck was a brown and white horse, with all the leather and tack sitting on the ground beside him. I didn't know what to say and just stood there with my mouth open for a minute.

"Go on, he's yours all right. You have to take care of him though, cause he's not a toy. I'll teach you how to ride when it gets a little warmer outside in the spring," Justin told me.

I didn't say anything else. I just walked down the steps and went up to my horse and started to get friendly with him. Horses have a strong smell if you're not used to them, or at least this one did. I wrinkled my nose a little bit, but I was more than willing to put up with that. I found out later that he was really a present from Justin and Eileen both. Her parents raise horses on a big ranch in Magnolia, and that's where this one had come from.

Justin is a man who never overlooks anything, like I said earlier. He must have remembered me saying something about wanting a place where I could ride. Either that, or he just knew me that well already.

I got up on his back for a minute and they took some pictures, then we went and put him in the pasture. We took some pictures out there too, of all three of us standing together in front of the gate, with Justin on one side and Eileen on the other and me in the middle. She has one of those cameras with a delay button so the person taking the photo has time to be in it too. I still have those pictures too, up on my bedroom wall.

Eileen went home not long after that, so she could get back to Magnolia before it got too late. She stood on the front porch kissing Justin for like ten minutes before she left, though. I knew that's what they were doing even though I was back inside by then. I could see them through the front window. And no, I was *not* spying, but when they didn't come in right away I peeked out through the blinds long enough to see what was keeping them so long.

I thought about razzing him for it when he came back in, but I finally decided not to. He probably would have just laughed and asked me if I was jealous, and that would have embarrassed me all over again. He stood out there and watched until her truck disappeared through the trees, then he came back inside with that silly Santa Claus cap still parked on his head.

"Well, bubba, did you have a nice Christmas this year?" he asked me after he shut the door.

"It was the best," I told him.

"I'm glad, then," he said.

We didn't say much more, cause it was getting late and we were both sleepy. I put on some shorts and an old t-shirt and crawled up under the covers on my top bunk, and laid there for a little while looking at the ceiling not far above my head. It was white, with little whorls in the paint that made it look almost like clouds.

I heard Justin singing something to himself in the kitchen, but it was too low for me to tell what it was. In a minute he came in and climbed up the bunk ladder part way to make sure I was warm enough and to say goodnight. He always did that much, so it didn't surprise me. What did surprise me a little was when he tucked the covers around my neck and then kissed me on the forehead before he climbed down to go to bed.

I guess everybody was handing out kisses that night.

After he left I touched my forehead with one hand. The skin still tingled a little where his stubbly goatee had scraped against it. It reminded me of something Daddy might have done a long time ago when I was little. It made me feel safe, like I always used to back then.

I went to sleep not long after that, happier than I'd been in a long time. You might say I had everything I ever wanted, and I knew I'd never have to worry about becoming a monster ever again. Justin and Eileen seemed to think the world of me, and what more could a kid ask for than that?

Well, there was *one* other thing, and I guess you probably know what it is before I even tell you. I had to let Mama and Daddy know I was all right. I didn't want them to worry about me.

That took some careful thinking, cause I sure didn't want to get Justin in trouble and I for double sure didn't want Mama and Daddy to know where I was at. So that meant I couldn't call, and I couldn't send a letter, and I guess standing on top of the truck and yelling probably wouldn't do much good either, would it?

I finally figured it out, even though it took me a few days to hit on the answer. That boy sitting across the aisle from me in the bus station in Fort Smith is what gave me the clue. I was thinking back over everything that had happened, like I did sometimes, and I remembered him using Yahoo Messenger that day.

As soon as I thought about it, I knew that was the answer to my problem. There was no way to trace an instant message as far as I knew, and Mama used Yahoo all the time. I could talk to her that way and she wouldn't be able to tell where I was unless I slipped up and told her something. I hoped I was smarter than that.

So I got online and signed in to my old account that she set up for me last spring. I almost never remembered the password, but I got it right on the third try. Then I sent Mama a message. She wasn't on right then, but I knew she'd get it when she did sign in. She never went more than a few days without talking to her friends.

I told her I was okay and I was in a good place where I'd be safe. I said I was happy and that I had to leave because I didn't want to be a *loup-garou*. I told her to tell everybody I loved them and please not to look for me, but I'd come back to visit someday when I could.

I didn't know what else to say, and it was harder than I thought it would be. But I read the message one last time, decided it was good enough, and clicked the send button.

Then I waited.

I checked my messages a lot over the next few weeks, and you know, I never did get an answer from her. I knew she would have gotten the message by that time, so at first I thought maybe she just didn't know what to say. At least that's what I told myself for a while.

It bothered me a little bit. I was expecting her to be mad at me, or to beg me to tell her where I was or to come home or something like that. I was ready for any of those reactions, and I thought I could handle them. But getting totally ignored left me confused and more than a little hurt. I wasn't sure what to think. It might have bothered me more, if I hadn't been thinking so much about something else those next few weeks.

Right after New Year's, Justin put me back in school, but not the kind I was used to. He started me out in a little private Christian school not far from the house. I think he had to, since he didn't have my birth certificate and all that other bull which a regular school always wants, and there was no way to get any of it right then. The owner of the school he picked for me was a friend of Eileen's and so they were a little more laid back about stuff like that.

It was close enough that I could walk or ride The Beast if I wanted to, and on rainy or cold days Justin usually took me himself. There were only four other kids in my class, which was way smaller than I was used to. But other than that it wasn't especially different than my old school. We studied math and history and science and all that good stuff just like I always had. We played football every day at lunchtime, and I made some good friends and got used to things soon enough.

Well. . . I have to admit there was *one* big difference between that place and my old school. We talked about God all the time, in every class. I learned more about that subject in a week than I'd ever heard before in my whole entire life, and that's what it was that had me doing so much thinking right then.

When I first went there, I hadn't made up my mind for sure if God even existed, much less what I thought he was like if he did exist. I can't say I never wondered about it at all before, but it wasn't something I'd spent tons of time thinking about, either. And it wasn't that anybody pushed me about it even then. They just told me things, and if I asked a question they answered it, and then they left me to make up my own mind.

There's no specific moment I can lay my finger on and say that's when I decided to believe, but I know when the day was. I was sitting on the dock by the lake, fishing with Eileen one Sunday afternoon during Spring Break. It was warm and sunny that day, with a little breeze making ripples across the water. I can't remember where Justin was that day, but me and Eileen were pretty tight by then. I found out she's a good fisherman. She could sweet-talk a bass out of the water on days when nobody else could have done it.

Anyway, if you had asked me that morning what I thought about Jesus, I would still have said I wasn't sure. But when I came back from the lake, if you'd asked me the same question, then I would have called him savior and King.

I'm not sure why particularly then. I wasn't thinking much about it while we were fishing. I was thinking more about the warm sun and the cool water on my bare feet, and talking to Eileen about horses and stuff, and watching the breeze blow her hair back. I remember she forgot to bring a pony tail holder that day, and her long hair kept tickling my face when the wind blew it that way.

Sometimes something grows and grows in your heart like a drop of water getting bigger and bigger on the lip of a faucet, and finally it gets big enough to fall. That's the best way I can describe how it happened.

However it was, I'm thankful.

Epilogue

All that was six months ago, and now I'm sitting here on my porch in Arkansas, looking out over the lake and fixing to go feed and water Buster and maybe brush him down. I can ride well enough not to fall off anymore, even though it took a few weeks of being really sore to learn how.

When Justin gets home in a little while, we might go riding around the lake before it gets dark, and I think Eileen might come over tonight and make us a shepherd's pie for supper, if I ask her just right. She's a really good cook when she has time to be.

Justin tells me they're getting married this fall, and then she'll come live here with us all the time. And I say the sooner the better. Anybody who can run a kitchen like that girl can, she definitely gets my vote.

There are times when I still want to chew on the past like a dog with an old bone, going over it in my mind again and again till I'm sick of it. I'm not sure it even helps much, but it's been hard sorting out how I feel about everything.

Justin was the one who said I should write down this whole story of what happened from the very beginning, and if I did then maybe I'd understand things better and have an easier time letting go. I didn't believe him at first, but I decided it was worth a try. It took longer than I thought it would and I found out you have to think about things in a different way when you're telling a story to somebody else than when you're just brooding about it. That by itself helped a lot.

He also told me awhile back that everything happens for a reason, and read me a verse from the Bible about how all things work together for good to those who love the Lord, even the really bad things. Then he said he was sorry about me having to run away, but he loved me and he was glad God brought me to live with him.

That was something I really needed to hear, and it probably did more good than anything else he could have said. I'm sure he knew that when he said it. He understands me so well.

Eileen tells me things like that too, but she has a little bit different personality than he does. Justin loves me like the sun loves the green grass; warm hearted and kind as springtime, always ready to play or listen to how I feel. Eileen is more like the ground under my feet, steady and sure, more practical and not quite so much of a dreamer.

You might say he's the one who builds castles in the sky and she's the one who puts the foundations under them. If you want to figure out how you feel and what you want and the things that will make you happy, then you go to Justin. If you want to figure out how to make those things happen in the real world, then it's better to ask Eileen.

I love them both so much.

I wonder sometimes about Lola, and what will happen to her when she gets older. I guess she'll have to make her own choices then about what she wants to do. Maybe by the time she's ten or twelve she'll be curious enough to want to find me and ask me why I left, and maybe by then I'll know the right words to tell her. I pray about that an awful lot.

I still haven't heard anything from mom and dad, even though I sent them several more messages. I guess they don't want to talk to me anymore or have anything to do with me since I don't want to be a monster.

I think I always sorta knew that's how it would be, deep down. I just didn't want to admit it to myself for a long time. I won't pretend it doesn't still hurt me sometimes. I cried a lot at first, till I learned to accept it.

But Justin loves me just the way I am, and so does Eileen, and so does God, and that's all I need to know.

The End

Enjoy this free sample of

Behind Blue Eyes
The Last Werewolf Hunter, Book Two

*All things work together for good to those who love God,
Who are called according to His purpose.*
-Romans 8:28

Chapter One

They caught me on a night when the moon was full, just like I always knew they would.

It was late September, and if you took a deep breath you could catch the first taste of fall in the air. I love that time of year, and that's why I went down to the lake that night to toss pebbles in the water and watch the ripples wash the shore. Justin and Eileen were at a conference in Houston, so I had the whole place to myself for the weekend.

Maybe I should have known better than to go traipsing down there alone on a full moon night, but it had been a long time since I ran away from home, almost two years in fact, and I guess I was starting to get careless. Besides that, I wasn't expecting anything to happen right there in my own back yard.

Not till the dude grabbed me, anyway.

Without a snarl or a growl, or even so much as a crunch of dead leaves under his feet to give me any warning, somebody snatched me from behind and slapped his hairy paw across my mouth to keep me from yelling.

Oh, I fought like a tiger on crack, but it didn't do me any good. I had one arm free and I used it to yank loose the silver cross I always wore around my neck for just such an emergency. It was made with a sharp point at each end, and as soon as I got hold of it I swung my hand up and nailed the dude right on the forearm. You might not think it sounds like much of a weapon, but for me a sharp piece of silver was better than all the guns and knives in the world.

The man cursed, and I think he almost let go of me for a second. I felt his hold loosen up just a little bit, but not quite enough for me to break free. Instead I felt a sharp little prickle in my side where his other arm was wrapped around me, right under my ribs. At first I thought it was a knife, but then I found out later it was a shot of horse tranquilizer.

I had time to be surprised that the silver hadn't done anything to the man, and I remember wondering what went wrong. Then everything went black.

* * * * * * *

I woke up with a pounding headache inside a dark stuffy place that smelled like wet dirt. I wasn't thinking too clearly yet, and the first thing that crossed my mind was that I was inside a coffin. That was such a horrible idea that I screamed, or at least I tried to. That's when I found out my mouth was covered with duct tape.

My hands and feet were taped up, too, and that's an awfully scary way to wake up, if you've never tried it. For a little while, terror threatened to drown out everything.

I took a deep breath and forced myself to calm down, though. I might be packed like a sardine in a can, but I was still alive and I didn't seem to be hurt except for the headache. My hands were taped together at the wrists, but I could still move my arms. I reached up and felt the ceiling, which was no more than a foot above my face. It felt like cardboard, and there was enough give that I could tell it wasn't a coffin at least. Not that I've ever actually been inside a coffin before, you know, but I was willing to bet they didn't make them out of cardboard. Nobody is *that* cheap and tacky.

That did wonders for my nerves, and I started to explore the situation a little better. The first step to getting yourself out of a pinch is to find out exactly what you're up against.

Whoever taped me up must have been in a hurry, because they were awfully careless about it. If they'd thought to tape my arms down to my sides then I probably would have been out of luck, but as it was I had some wiggle room. I brought my hands up to my face and pulled the tape off my mouth first, and then I started gnawing on the strip around my wrists.

Duct tape glue is really nasty, just in case you ever wondered. I wouldn't advise chewing on it unless you absolutely have to. It gets stuck in between your teeth and I think they must flavor it with dirty motor oil, the way it tastes. I felt like gagging.

It took me a good long time to chew my hands free. The tape tore hair off my wrists when I pulled it loose and I gritted my teeth from the pain. I didn't dare make noise, though, so I had to pull slowly even though it made it hurt more.

As soon as I could, I felt in my right jeans pocket where my cell phone should be. It was still there, so I flipped it open and used the backlight from the screen to look around. I was definitely inside a cardboard box, just like I thought; one that was barely big enough to hold me. There was some half-dried red clay mud on the walls down close to my feet, which must have been where the wet dirt smell had been coming from.

I tried to call Justin or Eileen, but all I got was a "call failed" message. Wherever I was, there was no cell service. I didn't waste time crying over it, though; I just closed the phone and slipped it back in my pocket. I didn't want to run the battery down when I might need it later.

As it turned out, I still had my pocketknife and my billfold and all my other stuff, too. The only thing missing was the silver cross from around my neck, and I might have dropped that on the ground when the man knocked me out. I felt almost naked without it.

I strained my ears to hear the slightest noise, but it was quieter than a cave in there. No engine or traffic sounds, no machinery, no voices, nothing.

I finally decided it was stupid to wait around for the man with the hairy hands to come back and find me. I had to get out of that box.

I pushed up with my palms, but the lid would only move a little bit before it stopped firmly. It was probably taped shut on the outside or some such thing, but I was ready for that.

I opened the little blade on my knife and stuck it into the side of the box way up high, and then sliced down in one smooth cut. You should never let your knife get dull, you know. You can never be sure when you might need it. You might never get trapped inside a cardboard box, but then again you never know. Just a few hours ago I never would have seen it coming myself. I always sharpened both blades at least once a week, and right then I was glad I did. I made two more quick cuts and then knocked out a piece of cardboard about twelve inches square.

The first thing I saw when I got the hole open was a spare tire lying flat on some dirty gray carpet, and the back of a leather car seat. I couldn't see much more than that because of the angle.

There was darned little room to move around inside that box, and I had to struggle a while and nearly scraped an ear off on the edge of the hole, but eventually I was able to push my head out to get a better look around. I was in the back cargo hold of a Bronco or a Blazer or something like that. The box I was in was tied up with plastic cords, just like I thought. Good enough.

I quickly sliced another cut in the box to make the hole bigger, and then wormed the rest of my body out.

The windows were tinted really dark, but it was daylight outside and I could see well enough. There wasn't much out there except a dirt road lined with thick pine trees behind me, and in front there was what looked like a deer camp. There were five or six cinder block buildings of pretty good size, and two other cars parked not far away. I was close enough to the nearest building to see dew still glistening and steaming on the metal roof, so it couldn't be very late yet. There was nobody in sight, but I knew better than to hang around. Somebody might show up any second.

I checked real quick to make sure there were no keys in the car. I knew that was probably too much to expect, but you never know. People are careless sometimes.

Oh, I don't really have my license yet, by the way, but I do know how to drive when I need to. Justin lets me drive the truck now and then on back roads where there's no traffic. I'd never tried to drive anything alone yet, but I figured this was an emergency and nobody would blame me for doing whatever I had to do.

No keys, though, so I gave up on the idea of driving away. Instead, I eased open the back hatch of the Blazer just enough to slither out, and then shut it again as quiet as a whisper. If I had to walk then that's what I'd do.

I was barefooted and that complicated things, but I knew I couldn't stay on the road. That was the first place they'd look when they found me gone. I wasn't thrilled with the idea of walking through the briers and rocks with no shoes on, but it looked like I didn't have much choice. So I took a deep breath and trotted off into the woods as fast as my feet could take me.

I didn't think anybody had seen me, but of course I couldn't be sure. For the next hour or so I didn't slow down for a second, even though I never heard anybody coming after me. I knew enough to head straight toward the sun so I wouldn't start walking in circles. I didn't want to run around all day and then end up right back at the camp again. Following the sun would keep me going in a straight line, at least. But as for where in the world I was, that was a whole 'nother question.

I checked now and then to see if my phone had service yet, but it never did.

The land was really steep and rocky in places, and that slowed me down. You can't climb as fast as you can walk, and the rocks were hard on my bare feet, just like I knew they would be.

After a while I came to a rocky stream, and I stopped to wash my sweaty face and take a drink. It looked like it was going to be another bull-roaster kind of day. September is like that now and then; it can still be hotter than a hen in a wool sweater, some days. I couldn't help wishing this hadn't been one of those times, but there was nothing I could do about it. In the meantime the creek was clear and cold, and the water tasted delicious to a boy who was almost dying of thirst by then. I splashed some of it on the back of my neck and my arms, and then I sat down on a big gray boulder and dangled my sore feet in the current. It felt so good I didn't want to get up.

But I knew I wasn't out of danger yet, and I didn't dare just sit and wait for Hairy Paws to come scoop me up. If he was a good enough tracker or if he had dogs then he could probably still follow my trail through the woods and catch me. I wasn't sure about that, and when you don't know then you don't take chances.

The little creek flowed somewhere off to the south, and I decided to follow it for a while. If you're lost in the woods, that's almost always a good idea. A flowing stream will usually lead you to people sooner or later. It also keeps you from getting lost and gives you water to drink, and you don't leave any trail or any scent to follow.

Daddy taught me all those things, back when we still used to talk about stuff sometimes, and for just a second I was grateful to him for that. Then I remembered he probably only did it to make me a better werewolf someday, and that wrecked the whole thing and left a sour taste in my mouth and for a while I almost hated him.

Justin would have told me to let it go and love him for whatever good there was in him, but that's hard, you know. It's easy to get bitter when somebody does you so much wrong, and every time I thought I was over it, little things like that kept reminding me at the weirdest times.

I decided not to think about it right then.

I slogged down the creek for several hours, and watched it get gradually bigger. The land was awfully mountainous, and I'm not sure how I could ever have made my way through if I hadn't had the stream. There were lots of little waterfalls about three or four feet high, but I could jump over those if I was careful. It was hot work doing all that hiking, and those occasional dunks kept me cool. I was hungry enough to gnaw the bark off the trees, but there was nothing I could do about that.

After a while, I came to a bridge.

Well, sort of. It was just a little foot bridge that crossed over the creek, and there were some picnic tables and a sidewalk on the left bank. It looked like a little park or some such thing, but there wasn't a soul to be seen.

Somebody had mowed the grass around the picnic tables not more than two or three days ago, and there was a Styrofoam cup still sitting on one of them, still half full of somebody's old coffee. When I nosed around a bit more I found a parking area, and then a dirt road that led away from it.

For a while I couldn't make up my mind whether to take a chance on the road or to keep following the creek a little farther downstream. The coffee cup and the mowed grass made me think this was a place where people visited fairly often, so after a lot of thinking I decided maybe the road would be a better choice.

Before I left the campground or park or whatever it was, I scrounged an empty plastic Coke bottle from the trash can and rinsed it out several times before filling it up at the creek. I knew I'd get thirsty and there was no telling the next time I'd come across any water.

It wasn't all that long before the road came to a T-junction, and there was a sign posted. The left arrow said

Hwy 8 - 5 miles, and the right arrow said something about a lake. I don't remember exactly, because as soon as I saw that highway sign I didn't care what might be in the other direction. I turned left.

The sign forgot to mention that the road ran steeply uphill most of the way, but I can promise you I noticed. It took me about three or four hours, but eventually I did make it to the highway with no particular trouble, except for my feet. They were killing me by then from walking barefoot on those gravel roads. They eat up your skin like sandpaper.

When I got to the highway there was no sign to tell me which way to go, so I shrugged and went east. It kept the sun out of my face, and I figured that was as good a reason as any.

I felt pretty good about things at that point. It seemed like the worst was behind me. I was tired and hungry and uncomfortable in other ways, but that was okay. I could probably thumb a ride to the nearest town, and then I could call Justin and have him come get me. And in the meantime while I waited for him to get there, I still had nineteen dollars in my pocket. I was looking forward to a nice juicy cheeseburger. It's amazing how delicious food is when you haven't eaten in a while.

So I stuck out my thumb whenever I heard a car coming, and waited for somebody to pick me up. Hitchhiking is kind of a chancy business, you know. You can never be sure who might stop, and there are some very strange people in the world to say the least. But right then I was ready to make friends with just about anybody.

That highway might have been built on the moon for all the cars I saw, but no matter how far out in the woods it is, every road has at least a little traffic. Two or three cars blew right past me without stopping, which is about what I expected. But after a while, a green Mustang with Alabama plates pulled over not far in front of me.

I hobbled up as fast as I could on my sore feet, and opened the door and sat down. The air conditioner was running, and the cold air inside felt wonderful. It was a girl driving, which sort of surprised me. Girls don't usually stop for anybody, but maybe she thought I was young enough to be harmless.

"You look like you could use a ride," she said with a smile.

"Yeah, I just need to get to the nearest store," I told her.

"Sure thing," she agreed. She had long blonde hair and she couldn't possibly have been more than twenty. I laid my head back on the seat and pretended to close my eyes since I didn't really want to talk, but she was so pretty I couldn't help watching her out of the slit of my left eye. She reminded me of someone I might have seen before, but I couldn't think who or where. It niggled at my mind like a gnat, till I finally decided it wasn't important.

A few miles down the road we went around a sharp curve, and she put both hands on the steering wheel to turn it. That's when I noticed what long, beautiful fingernails she had. Long, beautiful, *sharp* fingernails, perfectly manicured. Almost like claws, in fact. That's when I knew her for what she was.

My heart almost stopped, and I'm sure it came right up in my throat. I swear I could feel it sitting there on the back of my tongue. I don't think I could have said a word if my life depended on it.

I didn't let on. I kept pretending to rest while I thought desperately of how to get myself out of the hole I'd stepped into.

It was just barely possible that she didn't know who I was or have anything to do with me, of course. I knew how unlikely that was even while I was thinking it, but hope will make you grasp at straws and make a fool out of you if you're not careful. I knew I'd be crazy to believe she had nothing to do with me. That was way too much of a coincidence.

On the other hand, I was fairly sure she didn't realize (yet) that I knew she was a werewolf, and that gave me one slim advantage. She wouldn't be on her guard quite so much.

On the third hand, if she was specifically looking for me, there was no way she'd really take me to a store and drop me off, or even let me out of the car. Not unless I did some really smooth talking between now and then. I got a firm handle on my voice (I hoped) and opened my eyes with a fake yawn.

"So what's a pretty girl like you doing out here in the middle of nowhere?" I asked her with a smile. Eileen always tells me what a cute boy I am and what beautiful blue eyes I have, and I always used to laugh it off when she said such things, but if there was any chance it could help me then I was willing to give it a shot. Girls like all that flirty stuff for some reason, and I was betting this one was no different. She laughed a little.

"Oh, I'm just here with my family on vacation. Mom sent me to the store to get some ice and things," she said. It sounded reasonable, even though I didn't believe it for a second.

"You're from Alabama?" I asked.

"Yeah, Huntsville. Guess you saw my tags, huh?" she asked.

"Yeah, I did. Uh, so you're just going to the nearest store, then?" I asked, like I didn't care much.

"Yeah, but that's in Glenwood. The store in Norman doesn't have Cherry Dr. Pepper, and Mom won't drink anything else," she said glibly. I pounced on that.

"Would you mind very much if I rode to Glenwood with you? I know it's a lot to ask, but I'd really appreciate it," I said. I had to play things real carefully so I didn't make her suspicious. I wanted her to think she had me fooled. She probably wouldn't attack me as long as I wasn't putting up a struggle. It was a lot easier for her if I went along willingly as long as possible. The gloves would only come off when I tried to get away from her.

"Sure, I guess," she shrugged, "it's only a few extra miles."

"Thanks a lot. It's not every day you run into a girl as awesome as you," I told her, and smiled my best smile again. I was in danger of overdoing it, but all I can say is that I wasn't at my best at the time. Sitting next to somebody who could rip you to shreds with her bare hands makes it hard to think straight, believe it or not. The girl didn't seem to notice, though. She just laughed again.

"Yeah, that's what my boyfriend tells me all the time," she said. That's what I was expecting her to say, so I had that one covered.

"Well, dang. Lucky guy," I said, snapping my fingers. She smiled.

"Thanks anyway, honey. It was a sweet thing to say," she told me. I was pretty sure I had her fooled at that point, so I didn't push it any more.

Not long after that, we started passing a few houses and things, and it didn't look quite so deserted as it did before. We came to a junction and turned right, and I saw a gas station up ahead a few blocks. That's what I'd been waiting for, and it was time to make it or break it. I crossed my fingers and prayed for it to work.

Chapter Two

"Hey, could we make a pit stop at that gas station for just a second? I'm starving," I asked her. She didn't look really happy with that idea, but as long as we were still playing the game it was hard for her to say no. She tried, though.

"Do you think it could wait till we get to Glenwood?" she asked reluctantly.

"Well, see. . . if I don't eat then I get car sick really bad. I promise it won't take but a minute," I squeaked, doing my best to look as sick as possible. That almost always works, and this girl was no exception. Her eyes opened wide and she pulled over in front of the gas station right away. Nobody likes to get vomit in their car.

I opened the car door and walked into the station, which had a hole in the wall convenience store on one side. As soon as I was sure the girl couldn't see me, I took out my cell phone and tried to call Justin again, only to find that I still didn't have any service. I texted him instead just on the off chance that he might get it later.

I bought a Coke and some Cool Ranch Doritos since I really *was* dying of hunger, and when I paid for them I brought up the subject with the clerk.

"Uh, can I use the phone, ma'am? It's really important," I asked her.

"Is it a local call?" she asked. I knew that was coming.

"No, but I'm willing to pay for it. I'll give you five bucks," I said, pulling out the cash. The sight of money has a wonderful way of motivating people sometimes.

"Well, you can use mine if you want to, but keep it short if you can," she told me, handing me her cell phone. I noticed she used a different company than mine, but that was okay. That was probably why she had service and I didn't. I called Justin as fast as I could push the buttons.

All I got was his voicemail, but that didn't surprise me much. He was still at that dadgummed conference, and he'd probably be in and out of seminars where he couldn't get to his phone all day long. I left him a message saying I was at a gas station in Norman, Arkansas, and asked him to come get me. I couldn't say much more than that, not with the clerk standing right there in front of me. She'd think I was loony. I figured Justin was smart enough to fill in the blanks well enough, anyway. He'd know if I asked him to come all the way from Houston to pick me up, there'd have to be a really good reason for it. I told him to hurry as fast as he could and I'd call him back later when I had a chance to. Then I gave the girl back her phone and the five dollars.

I got one other thing while I was there, too. They had a rack of souvenir items against the wall, and amongst the postcards and shot glasses and assorted trinkets, I found something better than I dared hope for: a set of red heart-shaped ear rings with a ceramic bass in the center. I guess they were supposed to mean *"I love bass fishing"* or something like that. They were perfect!

No, I do *not* wear them, but the reason I wanted them was because they had sterling silver posts. It said so, right there on the label. They were $8.95 and that just about cleaned me out, but it was well worth it. Now I had a powerful weapon to use.

There was a garage attached to the store where they changed tires and things like that, so I went that way and walked out the back of the building so the girl in the car wouldn't see me leave. I'm pretty sure I wasn't supposed to use the back door, but nobody said anything.

As soon as I got outside I hurried away, being sure to keep the gas station between me and the Mustang for as long as I could. While I walked I tore the ear rings open and dropped the extra one in my pocket while I held the other one in my hand. I wanted to be ready to defend myself if I had to.

I quickly found out there aren't too many places to hide in Norman, and I started to get a little scared again. I didn't dare stay out in the open for too long. Before very much longer Blondie would figure out I'd slipped the noose, and then she'd be after me. She'd probably be furious, too, and there'd be no fooling her next time if she caught me again.

I spied a bridge over a little river and made a beeline for that, walking as fast as I could without running. If you start to run then people get curious, and I didn't want anybody to remember seeing me.

I made it to the bridge in double quick time, and ducked underneath it after glancing around to make sure nobody was watching. There were a lot of big gray rocks under there and a little bit of sandy beach down next to the water, so it wasn't too bad of a place to hole up for a while. I climbed way up near the top where it was harder for anybody to see me, and there I sat.

I tore into the chips and the coke while I had time, and I don't think anything ever tasted so good.

Hiding under a bridge like a troll in a fairy tale was not the best plan in the world, I have to admit, but it was the only thing I could think of right then.

Now and then I heard cars passing by on the bridge over my head. They made the whole bridge shake and rattle around me like it was about to fall apart any second, but none of them stopped. The girl in the green car must have figured out I'd flown the coop by then, and I was willing to bet she was hot on my heels. Others too, most likely. Back up on the roads was the last place on earth I needed to be.

I moved downhill a little bit so the bridge didn't make so much noise when cars went by, and then I sat there tossing pebbles into the water for a while and thinking about what I should do. The river was clear and blue, gurgling and splashing over gravel bars and rocks, but it was no more than about waist deep. It was hot even in the shade, and the water looked inviting to say the least. I wished it was just an ordinary day and I could jump in for a swim.

I noticed an old river tube caught in the debris under the bridge stanchions, and that gave me an idea. There was *one* way I could get far away without being seen on the roads, if I could make it work.

I picked my way down to the bank, then waded out there to look at the tube a little closer. Sure enough, it had a hole in it about the size of a pencil, but it seemed otherwise okay. A holey tube won't do you much good for long, but it might work just long enough to save my bacon, if I played my cards right.

I stuck my left thumb in the hole to plug it, then started to blow up the tube with my mouth. I left it a little bit loose and flabby on purpose so there would be less chance of leaking, and waited a minute to see whether it held air. It seemed to be holding steady for the moment at least, and I decided to risk it. If it blew out on me later, I could always swim if I had to.

The water was shallow enough that I could climb into the tube without too much trouble, so I clumsily got into the seat while trying to leave my thumb plugging the hole. It wasn't easy to twist myself around and find a comfortable spot, but I finally managed it. Then I paddled out into the current as best I could with one hand. Before long the stream grabbed me, and away I went at a pretty good clip.

Floating a river is fun, if you've never tried it. I'd done it lots of times with Justin and Eileen. Not usually in a leaky tube, to be sure, but as long as it held air I was okay with it. The late afternoon sun sparkled off the water, which was just a tad bit chilly but not too cold to handle. If it had been very much later in the year I wouldn't have been able to stand it, but as it was I didn't mind so much.

I wrapped up my phone in the empty Doritos bag from the gas station, rolling it up as tight as I could to keep it from getting wet. I could brush the chip crumbs off later, but phones don't handle water too well.

I thought I knew where I was, now. I'd been to Norman once before to go digging for quartz crystals and to float this very river for a few miles. At least I thought it was the same river. It had been a year or so ago, but the more I thought about it the more certain I was. I was maybe a hundred miles or so from home. I just needed to head south, and that's the way the river would take me anyway for now.

The Caddo River doesn't really have what you'd call whitewater, exactly. Just a few little riffles and such, not enough to even pay attention to. I remembered that much. I'd been in a canoe the last time I was here, but it shouldn't make much difference. I had to keep an eye out for logs and rocks and willow strainers, and that's about it. With a bit of luck, it would carry me all the way to Glenwood.

I'd have to get out of the water there and start watching my back again. The river didn't go much farther before it fed into Lake Degray, and then there wouldn't be any current to carry me anymore. So, Glenwood it would have to be.

Blondie probably didn't have a clue where I was right that minute, but she might very well guess where I was headed, especially since it was the only close town. She surely knew where I lived, and she probably also knew there was no other way for me to get there except by going through Glenwood. Not without going forty or fifty miles out of the way, and I didn't have time or money for that. There were mountains all around, and the river and the highway followed the one and only gap through them. She'd be watching that place like a hawk on a mouse-hole.

But for the meantime I was safe from prying eyes, so I relaxed and laid my head back on the tube and closed my eyes. I knew better than to go to sleep, but I wanted to think.

Who were these people that seemed so bent on catching me, and what did they want? I knew the girl was a werewolf; her fingernails gave that away, and it was hard for me to believe she wasn't connected with the people at the deer camp. But on the other hand, why hadn't my silver cross done anything to the man who caught me in my own back yard? That made me wonder if maybe he *wasn't* one. But if not, then why was he helping them? And again, what did they want with me?

That's the one thing I kept coming back to. Why me? And why now? I had wolves in my family, sure, but I hadn't seen or talked to them in two years. No one had ever bothered Justin just because his sister was a *loup-garou*, so why should it matter if my parents were? What did they want?

Try as I might, there was no way I could figure that one out. Not unless I found out more, and I didn't know any way of doing that right now.

The river gurgled and whispered to itself, and the quiet and the solitude were starting to make me sleepy. I raised my head to shake loose the cobwebs; it would never do to fall asleep in the tube and then hit a log or a rock and get dumped in the river with no warning a split second after waking up. That was a good way to lose my tube in the current or even drown.

The rest of the afternoon passed without too much to say about it. The banks glided by smoothly and swiftly, and the occasional riffle was no trouble. Every now and then I had to blow some more air into the tube when it got too flabby. I almost got tangled up in a willow strainer once, at a place where the current passed close to the bank and tried to pull me right under a thicket of low-hanging branches. I had to paddle hard with my right hand to keep from getting sucked in there.

After a few hours I passed a place where the bank had been turned into a parking lot, and I felt the water turn suddenly warm around me right through there, which startled me. I guess there was a hot spring under the water or some such thing. It felt nice, but after I passed through it and got back into the ordinary water it only reminded me how cold I was. I thought again about how it was really too late in the year to be floating like this.

There were some people lounging around on the tailgate of a red pickup truck in the parking lot, and they seemed to think it was way too cold to be out there on the river, too.

"You're gonna freeze your butt off, boy!" they called out cheerfully. They meant well, so I didn't take offense.

"Nah, I'm all good!" I yelled back, just as cheerfully. They laughed and waved me off. I didn't mind the conversation so much, but what did make me uneasy was that I could see the highway the whole time I was in that little area. Anybody driving by could have seen me on the river just by turning their head.

That didn't happen, though, and it wasn't more than a few minutes till I floated under another bridge and back into the woods again. It only seemed like a week.

By that time I was getting really tired of riding on that dadgummed tube, and dusk was coming on pretty fast, too. It wouldn't be more than thirty minutes till the stars came out. Any other time I wouldn't have even thought about staying out on the river after dark, and certainly not without at least the moon. It was way too dangerous.

But as it was, I was probably safer on the water than I was on the road. The moon would be up in an hour or so, and as long as I kept my eyes peeled and my ears pricked and paid attention to what was around me, it would probably be okay.

I hoped.

And so it was. I won't say I enjoyed it much, but I've gone through worse things. After a long time I saw another big highway bridge up ahead and a bunch of yellow and red canoes down below it on the left bank. There was a shallow gravel bar where I ran aground on purpose, and then I clambered my way out of the river like a waterlogged rat. I was shivering by then and being wet didn't help, but there wasn't much I could do about it.

I climbed up the bank and came to the highway, then scooted across an old football field till I got to a Wright's grocery store. I couldn't go inside soaking wet and with no shoes on, unfortunately. They kinda frown on that, even in Arkansas.

Instead, I went behind the store beside the trash dumpster and took off my shirt and wrung as much water out of it as I could, and then I did the same thing with my shorts. It felt weird getting buck naked in a public place like that, I have to say. It was fairly dark behind the store, but still. If anybody had come waltzing around the corner right then I think I would have died three times before I could hit the concrete.

I was still damp after I finished, but at least I was dry enough not to drip river water all over the place. There was nothing I could do about my bare feet, so I decided I'd just have to brazen it out. Maybe they wouldn't say anything to me about it if I didn't draw attention to myself.

So I breezed inside like I owned the place and got me a turkey and cheese sandwich and paid for it with almost the last of my change. That one bag of chips hadn't done much for me, and even that was hours and hours ago. Nobody said anything about my feet.

I went back outside and ate my food, and that's when I found out my cell phone was soaked. The water must have got in at some point, in spite of the Doritos bag. I shouldn't have been surprised, I don't guess. I sighed and wiped it as dry as I could on my shirt tail. There was a chance it might work again after it dried out. Sometimes they do.

There was a pay phone in front of the grocery store, and I still had fifty cents left in my pocket. I walked over there and tried to call Justin one more time. All I got was his voicemail again, but I let him know I was in Glenwood at the grocery store and he needed to come get me as soon as he could. I told him everything this time, since there was nobody around to hear what I was saying.

That's when I got careless. Instead of finding somewhere to hole up and hide for a while, like I should have done, I went back and sat down on the bench in front of the grocery store. I don't know what I was thinking, looking back. Maybe somewhere in the back of my mind I had the notion that Justin might try to call the payphone back or something like that. I don't know what I thought, honestly. But I was bone tired, and I felt safe at that point, and so I stupidly sat there in a public place in full view of the highway. I could kick myself for it, but there you go.

After a while, a dark blue Blazer pulled into the parking lot, and I paid no attention even when it circled slowly around the lot and came near the front of the store. Sometimes people do that, you know, when they're looking for a parking spot close to the doors. I think they probably waste more time circling the lot than they would if they just walked all the way.

Anyway it was late and so this one found a spot pretty close to the front, and three or four people got out. It was too dark for me to see them very well or I might have thought one of them looked awfully familiar, but as it was I didn't notice.

One of them pulled something out of her purse, and a second later I felt a sharp sting when something hit me in the chest. I just barely had time to look down and see a dart sticking out of my shirt, and after that everything went dark.

Chapter Three

I guess they carried me all the way back to the deer camp after they knocked me out, because when I woke up that's where I was again. Only this time I wasn't taped up in a cardboard box that I could cut my way out of. I was lying on a creaky old metal hospital bed, with my left wrist handcuffed to the bed frame.

"That's right; you won't get away so easy this time, you slippery little fish," the blonde girl from the car told me. She was standing at the foot of my bed, and there wasn't a trace of a smile on her lips now. She was probably right about that, I thought to myself, but I wasn't going to give her the satisfaction of seeing that I was afraid.

"Where am I?" I demanded, giving her the nastiest scowl I could manage. She did smile then, and it wasn't a very nice smile either.

"I don't see why I should tell you anything, Zach," she said. Somehow I wasn't surprised she knew my name, but I let it pass. She was trying to score points, and I wasn't going to play that silly little game with her.

"Fine, then. Don't tell me anything," I said calmly. I knew they wanted something from me, and that meant they'd have to tell me what it was sooner or later. All I had to do was wait, and she'd have to spill the beans whether she wanted to or not.

I could tell my answer annoyed her, but that was good. People will sometimes say things they didn't mean to say if you can get them riled up.

"The question you ought to be asking is *why* you're here, and there's no secret about that one. You're here to join us, and this time there won't be any last minute escapes," she said sweetly. I didn't have to ask her what she meant by that. I knew only too well.

That news rattled me a bit in spite of myself, and I couldn't resist asking her a question.

"But why? I already told everybody I didn't want anything to do with that stuff. I won't make trouble for anybody, I just want to be left alone," I told her.

"'Fraid it doesn't work that way, honey. Not for *you*, anyway," she added as an afterthought. That made me want to ask her what was so dadgummed special about *me*, but I saved that for later. When you're talking to an enemy you should never let them know what you're really interested in. It gives them the upper hand. I learned that from reading *The Prince* last year in English class. All that political intrigue and stuff bored me to tears at the time, but right now my tongue was the only weapon I had, so I figured I better make it count.

"You can't make me if I don't want to; I know how it works," I said, changing the subject.

"Maybe not, but if you ever want to leave here and go home then you'll agree. Otherwise. . . " she shrugged.

"You can't keep me here forever," I said.

"We can keep you as long as we need to, honey, and that's all that matters," she said, with another one of those hateful smiles.

Deep down, I was seriously afraid she might be right about that. Out in the middle of nowhere like this, who would there be to help me? Nobody, that's who. Justin thought I was in Glenwood, and what would he do when he got there and I was gone? I was sure he'd look for me, but it was the longest of long shots that he'd ever find me in a place like this. He wouldn't even be able to call the police to help. All they'd do would be to call my parents. Fat lot of good *that* would do me.

I thought about all that in the space of a few seconds, and I soon decided the only thing I could do right then was pretend to go along with it for a while. They wouldn't trust me, of course, but they might let their guard down enough to give me a chance to escape again. If I was sullen and resentful then that would never happen.

I changed my tack.

"So you're telling me if I agree to this, then you'll leave me alone and let me go home?" I asked.

"Sure, if that's what you want. But you won't, Zach. Not after you become one of us. I can promise you that," she told me confidently.

Now came the difficult part, so I picked my words carefully.

"Well. . . I *might* do it if it means I never have to deal with yall's ugly faces anymore, but there's something I want first," I finally told her. She frowned a little bit.

"You don't have a lot of room to ask for much, Zach," she said. Then she seemed to think better of it.

"But if it will get you to do this willingly, and if it's not too unreasonable, then we might be able to make a deal. What do you want?" she asked me.

That was just the opportunity I'd been waiting for. I didn't really want anything from them, of course; I was just playing for time. But I couldn't ask for something stupid or that would blow the whole thing. It had to be something they could believe I might really want, and hopefully something only they could give me. It couldn't be anything too easy or it wouldn't gain me any time, and it couldn't be too hard or they'd refuse. That sounds like a tall order, I know, but I thought I had the perfect thing in mind.

"I want to see my sister first," I told her. I could tell that wasn't something Blondie was expecting to hear, but she was good at hiding her surprise.

"I see," she finally said, half to herself. She thought about it for a while longer, seeming to chew it over in her mind.

Then she looked at me for a long time, like she was trying to decide if I was for real or not. Maybe it helped that in my heart of hearts I really did want to see Lola; I don't know. Whatever the reason, Blondie seemed like she made up her mind to go along with it, at least for the time being.

"I'll have to see about that before I give you an answer," she finally said. That was about what I thought she'd say, so I just nodded.

"In the meantime I'll let you loose for a little bit, but you better not try anything. There's no way out of this room except through the door, and you certainly won't get out that way. I suggest you be good this time. If we're going to start trusting each other then it needs to go both ways," she told me.

I tried to look very solemn and serious at that, but inside I was overjoyed. I didn't even crack a smile, though. If I did then she might not turn me loose.

She pulled a key from her pocket and unlatched the handcuffs that held me to the bed, then slipped them in her pocket along with the key. I sat up, rubbing my wrist where the metal had chafed it.

"See, we can be nice to each other instead of having to do things the hard way, can't we?" she asked.

I think I liked her less and less the more she talked, so I didn't say anything to that. I can't stand people who look down their noses at everybody and think they're so high and mighty, and Blondie seemed like exactly that kind of person.

She didn't wait for an answer, thankfully; just knocked on the door to have somebody on the other side let her out. I heard the snick of a heavy-duty lock when the door shut behind her.

As soon as her footsteps faded away down the hall, I jumped up and started to explore the room to see if there was any way out. I had no intention of waiting to see what her answer was about Lola. If I found a way to bust out of there, I meant to take it. I knew what they wanted now, and the worst they could do was catch me and lock me up again. I wouldn't be much worse off than I already was.

It didn't take me very long to eyeball the whole place, and I have to say things didn't look too good. The walls were plain cinder block, painted over with three or four layers of off-white paint, and the only windows were some narrow slits too high up on the walls to even see out of. I think a cat would have had a hard time squeezing through one of them. There was a rusty steel door that led into a bathroom, which had the same cinderblock walls and slitted windows as the main room.

For furniture there was nothing but the old metal hospital bed that looked like it came from a salvage yard. There were no sheets on the mattress, no pillow, and just a plain wool blanket to cover up with. The rest of the room was totally empty.

The floors were concrete, partly covered by some brown and white tiles that had come loose in places. The door that led outside into the hall was a big monster of a thing, metal except for a diamond-shaped window about the size of my palm. Just big enough for them to be able to look in and see what I was doing whenever they felt like it. There was no keyhole on my side of the door.

I sat down on the bed again and thought about it a while. I wasn't ready to give up just yet, but I was blessed if I could think of a way to get out of there.

Sometimes when you go stale on a problem, it helps to think about something else for a while. I might not be able to figure a way out of there just yet, but I could still chew on some other things I didn't have the answers to. Like why the wolves wanted me so bad, for one thing. There was something about me in particular that had their knickers in a knot, something which didn't apply to Justin or anybody else. Blondie had admitted that much. But what could it be?

Try as I might, I couldn't figure out anything all that special about me. It couldn't be because I might tell somebody about them. Nobody would believe me anyway, and besides that, Justin had known about them for years and nobody had ever kidnapped him or caused him any problems just because he knew too much.

So if it wasn't that, then what was it? That part still baffled me.

I laid back on the mattress and laced my fingers together behind my head, staring up at the ceiling while I thought. It was one of those ceilings with blown plaster all over it with little sparkly things embedded, and they glittered in the light from the windows.

After a while that ceiling gave me an idea. Plaster is tough, but it's nowhere near as tough as concrete blocks. I might be able to knock a hole in it, if I could find something to do it with and a place where nobody could see me.

I knew the main room would never do, because of that danged window in the door. Anybody might walk by and see what I was doing, at any time. Even if I took my shirt off and used it to cover up the window, I figured that would be a surefire way to make the wolves suspicious enough to open the door and come in there, and if they did then it would wreck everything.

There was still the bathroom, though. I got up and moseyed in there and shut the rusty door behind me. That took care of not being seen. Sure enough, it had the same kind of ceiling as the other room, and I glanced around to see if there was anything I could use to dig a hole in it.

That bathroom was about as bare as a picked bone, I have to say. There was absolutely nothing in it except the commode, a sink, the bathtub, and a metal medicine cabinet which turned out to be completely empty. Nothing sharp or useful at all.

I thought about breaking the mirror on the medicine cabinet or smashing the lid of the toilet tank against the floor to get a sharp piece I could use, but I didn't waste half a second giving up on those ideas. Smashing things would make way too much noise, and I didn't dare attract attention. I thought longingly of my pocket knife, or one of the ten million screwdrivers Justin had in his workshop. I think I would even have settled for a paperclip at that point.

My pockets were stripped empty this time, though. The wolves had taken everything I had except for a few pieces of lint.

I wasn't ready to give up yet, though. I took the lid off the toilet tank and looked inside there. Toilets have a couple of moving parts, and sometimes a few of them are metal.

Just as I thought, there was a thin metal rod that connected the floater thingy to the water valve. I stuck my hand down inside the tank and found that I could unscrew the whole thing from the valve if I twisted hard enough. It was slimy and nasty and hard to keep hold of, but after a few minutes I had the metal rod loose, with the floater still attached to one end of it. The floater was supposed to unscrew from the rod the same way, but it had been on there so long it wouldn't come free.

I finally gave up trying to get it off. I had one sharp end, and that's all I needed.

I put the lid back where it came from and then gingerly climbed up on top of the tank itself. It was none too sturdy, and I had to be careful not to move too much because every time I did, the tank swayed and wobbled and acted like it was about to dump me on the floor. I used one hand to steady myself against the medicine cabinet till I was sure I wasn't going to fall.

When I was sure, I took the floater rod and started scratching at the ceiling right above me. It's hard to dig a hole in gypsum board, but if you're determined and if you've got something halfway sharp, you can do it.

Plaster dust kept sifting down on my face and making me want to sneeze, but at last the rod poked clean through to the other side. I went after it with doubled energy after that, till I made a hole big enough to stick my thumb through. I hooked a finger around the back of the plaster and pulled down. It wouldn't break and I was afraid to put my weight into it. I didn't want to go crashing to the floor if it broke loose all of a sudden.

I attacked it with the rod again, working all around the edges till I could get my three middle fingers inside. Then I pulled with all my strength, and just when I thought I was about to give myself a hernia, a palm-sized piece of plaster broke loose in my hand.

"Awesome," I said to myself, whispering so nobody could hear me.

I set the piece of plaster on top of the medicine cabinet and started breaking off more pieces. After that it didn't take long at all before I had a hole in the ceiling big enough for me to stick my head through, and finally it was big enough for my whole body.

I stopped my demolition work and reached up to grab hold of two rafters with my hands, and then I pulled myself up till I could sit on one of them. The whole thing only took maybe thirty minutes.

I found myself in a crawl space not much more than five feet high. It was awfully dark up there, and blistering hot, too. I could see rafters stretching off for a long way in both directions, and there was a metal roof right above me that was giving off heat like a demon. I was already sweating.

There was no use trying to hide the hole in the ceiling, so I didn't bother. If anybody came in the bathroom then my goose was cooked, plain and simple. And I knew sooner or later somebody *would* come, if only to check on me. That's why I didn't have a second to waste.

I stood up as best I could and started stepping carefully from rafter to rafter. That was ticklish business, because I knew if I stepped in the wrong place I'd end up crashing down through the plaster into the room below me.

That didn't happen though, because every so often there were ventilation grates that opened into the rooms below. They let in just enough light so I could sort of see where I was going, after my eyes adjusted.

They let noises come up into the attic, too, and when I heard Blondie's voice I froze for a second. She was talking to somebody in the room right under me, in that same prissy, superior tone I hated so much.

At first I was tempted to ignore her and go on my way, but then I heard my name.

"You might as well go ahead and tell me, honey. Zach already decided to help us," I heard her say. Maybe I'm too curious for my own good, but I couldn't help wondering what it was I was supposed to be helping them with. It was certainly news to *me*.

I forgot all about trying to get out of the attic, at least for the moment, and crept a little closer to the vent and leaned down close where I could hear better. It was a long shot, but there was always the chance I might learn something useful.

I could see into the room a little bit, but not enough to catch a glimpse of the girl or who she was talking to. All I could see was the edge of the sink in the bathroom and a slice of the open door.

"Laura, you're such a liar. If Zach already told you where it is then you wouldn't still be asking *me*. But you're wasting your time, because I already told you fifty million times I don't know anything," I heard someone else say. It was a boy's voice, and he sounded a little bit younger than me. That was all I could tell.

Right after that, I heard the sharp smack of a hand against bare skin. There was no way of mistaking what it was. There's nothing quite like that sound.

"You're so stupid, Cameron. You could save yourself so much pain and trouble if you'd just cooperate. You know we'll find it anyway sooner or later," she told him.

"I told you I don't know where it is," he said, in a voice that maybe shook a little bit but still sounded very sure. I could imagine the girl gritting her teeth, and then she slapped him again for good measure.

"That's a taste for later," she hissed. He didn't answer, and after a few seconds I heard her walking across the tile floor away from me.

"I'll leave you to think about that for a while. I'll be back later to see if you've changed your mind," she told him. I heard the door open and then slam shut behind her, and then the room below me was quiet.

I wondered why she'd been so nice to me earlier, if this was the way she treated her other prisoners. Maybe she was just waiting to see if I could be talked into doing what she wanted, and she'd only get nasty when she decided being nice wasn't going to work.

I don't like it when I see people getting mistreated. It makes me mad, and I want to do something about it if I can.

I made a quick decision.

"Hey kid. . . Cameron," I called out, torn between wanting him to hear me and not wanting my voice to carry too far. I don't think he heard me, so I called again, a little louder. That time I heard the bed creak.

"Who's there?" he said out loud.

"Don't say anything. Just come in the bathroom," I told him. He must have wondered what was up, but he didn't argue about it. After a few seconds I saw a boy in bare feet and a ratty white t-shirt come into the bathroom. There was a red hand print on his left cheek where Laura had slapped him twice. He had blond hair and he wasn't as young as I thought he was. He looked about the same age as me, more or less.

"Look up here. At the vent," I told him. He didn't act surprised. Just shut the bathroom door behind him and looked up at me. He had bright blue eyes almost exactly the same color as mine, and I remember thinking it was unusual at the time. I doubted he could see me in the dark attic, so I stuck my hand down close to the grate and waved at him. He'd be able to see motion at least.

"Who are you, and what are you doing up there?" he asked, getting right to the point.

"I'm here to help you get out of this place if you want to," I told him.

"Yeah? How?" he wanted to know.

"I'll break the ceiling plaster and you can climb up here in the attic with me. Just make sure it doesn't make any noise when it falls," I warned him.

It didn't take him long to make up his mind.

"Sure, I'm game," he said.

He quickly climbed up on the tank lid just like I had, and stood there ready to catch any pieces that might fall. I put one foot on the plaster right about where I judged his head was, and then gradually put more and more of my weight on it till I felt it start to crack. I was careful to keep my other foot on a rafter and hold on with both hands to the roof struts so I wouldn't fall through the ceiling when it broke.

Which it finally did. My foot punched through and I almost kicked Cameron in the face, if he hadn't ducked just in time. No big pieces fell, just a few little globs that didn't make enough noise to matter. Cameron grabbed the edges of the hole and pulled down several big chunks of plaster, and as soon as that was done, I gave him a hand and hauled him up into the attic with me.

"Come on, let's find a way out of here," I said. Introductions and chit-chat could wait till later. The wolves might discover one of us missing at any time. Cameron nodded without saying a word, and I went back to feeling my way through the dark.

It wasn't long before we came to the end of the building. There was a wooden louvered window there to let air circulate into the attic, but it also gave us a chance to see outside without anybody being able to tell we were there.

I peered through the cracks and saw a few other buildings and a couple of cars, but no people moving around. None of the buildings seemed to have windows except for those same little slits like I'd seen in my room. Maybe that's because it was a deer camp and they wanted to keep people from breaking in through the windows during off-season; I really don't know for sure. Whatever the reason was, it was a good thing for me and Cameron. Even if there were people inside those other buildings, they wouldn't be able to see us even after we got outside. We needed every piece of luck we could get.

But in the meantime, there was no way to get out through those dadgummed louvers. They were nailed together tight, and unless we had a hammer they were going to stay that way.

"Are we getting out this way?" Cameron whispered.

"I don't think we can, without a hammer or somethin'. Come on and let's look for the door instead. There's got to be one here somewhere," I whispered back.

I knew there had to be an access panel or a trap door or some such thing, if we could just find it. People had to come up there for maintenance and stuff now and then, didn't they?

We were both sweating so much by then it was running down and getting into our eyes and making them sting, and my whole t-shirt was soaked. I couldn't see Cameron well enough to tell whether he was as bad off as I was, but I'd be willing to bet on it. It was so hot it was hard to breathe, and I knew neither one of us could handle that for very long. We'd pass out from heat exhaustion if we didn't find a way out soon.

By and by we stumbled across an area where the floor was finished out with plywood, and there were some boxes and things stacked up. There was a trap door off to one side which I guess led down to the main floor of the building, but when Cameron tried to open it we soon found out it wouldn't move an inch. Locked, I'm sure.

"This thing's not coming open, dude. It won't even budge," he told me.

We felt around the edges of the door to see if there was a key or a latch or anything else that might let us open the trap and get out, but there wasn't anything. I bet it was probably locked with a hasp and a padlock down below, because when you got to thinking about it, why would anybody ever need to unlock the door from the top side?

At that point I was frustrated and starting to get a little scared that we wouldn't be able to find a way out, after all. I even seriously started to think about breaking down through the ceiling somewhere into one of the other rooms and trying to sneak out through the front door.

That's when I found the pipe.

It was just a stick of galvanized metal water pipe, old and rusty and no particular use to anybody, I don't guess. You know how attics always collect junk like that which nobody really gives a hoot about but nobody ever wants to throw away. The pipe was about three feet long, and the only reason I found it at all in the pitch dark was because I stepped on it and nearly brained myself on the rafters when it rolled out from under my foot.

Luckily I caught my balance before I killed myself, and when I groped around on the floor to see what it was I'd stepped on, I felt the pipe. I grabbed it in my hand and picked it up.

At first the only thing I had in mind was to use it for a weapon to defend myself if I had to. A piece of steel pipe can make a mighty fine club, in a pinch. It took me a few minutes before I realized it could make a mighty fine pry bar, too.

Chapter Four

"Come on, Cameron, I've got an idea," I told him.

We picked our way back to the louvered window and I stuck the metal pipe in between the slats, real close to one edge where the nails were. Then I pulled.

The nails made a horribly loud squealing noise when they pulled out of the wood, and I stopped, my heart pounding. It was so loud I was sure somebody down below would hear it and come find us.

"What's wrong? Why'd you stop?" Cameron asked.

"It's too loud. Somebody's bound to hear the noise," I whispered.

"Well pull slower then, but we have to get that window open, dude. There's no other way out and we got no time to look for one," he pointed out.

I know good sense when I hear it, so I bit my tongue and yanked hard on the bar. The nails came squealing out of the window frame, and before long I had one end of the board free. Cameron grabbed it and twisted it loose on the other side, and then he set it down carefully. The nails were making enough racket without dropping pieces of wood on the floor.

We yanked off six more louvers as fast as the walrus opened oysters, and then we had a space plenty big enough for us to fit through. I gave it one more wary look to make sure there was nobody around outside before I tore the screen loose. I didn't care about fixing it later; I just punched a hole in it with the metal pipe and then ripped it the rest of the way open the best I could.

It was maybe ten feet to the ground, but that couldn't be helped. I put my feet through first and then my body, till I was standing on the outside of the windowsill.

It looked a lot farther down than it really was. Maybe that's just because I don't like heights very much, but this time I didn't have any choice. I took a deep breath and jumped.

With my eyes shut.

It kinda hurt when I landed, but I was ready for that. I dropped and rolled to take some of the force off my feet, so that helped. As long as I didn't twist an ankle I was good to go.

The first thing I did when I got outside was to slick myself right up against the wall of the building and look around to see if anybody had noticed me jumping out of the window.

I didn't see or hear anything unusual, so I relaxed just a tiny bit. To tell the truth, it felt so good to be out in the cool air after nearly roasting to death in that attic, it was hard to think of anything else. I took deep breaths and just gloried in it for a whole ten seconds before I remembered we weren't out of the woods just yet.

I waved to Cameron to come on down, which he did. He didn't land quite as well as I did and ended up tearing a hole in the knee of his jeans and skinning his left palm. I knew it had to hurt, but he joined me against the wall without saying anything about it.

"You okay, bud?" I asked.

"Yeah, I'm good. Just stings a little, that's all," he said. He took his shirt tail and pressed it against his palm so it would quit bleeding.

The dark blue Blazer was parked maybe twenty feet away at the corner of the building we were next to, and that gave me an idea.

We slid along the wall as smooth as a melted Mars bar, till we got up close beside the car. Then I stealthily reached up and grabbed the door handle, and when I tried it I found that it was unlocked.

I motioned for Cameron to get in, and then I slipped into the driver's seat behind him and shut the door without slamming it. Those dark-tinted windows helped a lot now, since it meant nobody could see us inside unless they came really close.

There was an insurance card clipped on the dashboard that said the Blazer belonged to somebody named Janelle Parker from West Memphis. I'd never heard of her, but you never could tell when it might turn out to be a useful little tidbit of information.

It was more than I'd dared to hope for, but this time the keys were sitting in the cup holder on the console. Whoever drove the Blazer last time wasn't as careful as he should have been. Maybe he didn't think there was any reason to be careful about leaving the keys lying around, not this far back in the woods and with me and Cameron locked up tight.

Good enough. I picked them up, a little nervous. Every vehicle handles a little bit different, and I'd never tried to drive anything this big and bulky before. So yeah, honestly I was more than a little nervous. Cameron looked at me skeptically.

"Are you sure you're okay to drive?" he finally asked.

"Sure, I can drive just fine," I promised. He didn't look like he was totally convinced, but he didn't say anything else about it. We were both barefooted, and I'm sure he didn't want to try to run off through the woods like that. I know I didn't. I remembered what it felt like the last time.

I stuck the key in the ignition and started the engine. It was a quiet one, thankfully, so I was pretty sure nobody could hear it. I pulled the door shut real slow till I felt the lock click, and then I put the Blazer in reverse and backed up till I had enough room to clear the corner of the building. The brakes were touchier than I was used to and I skidded on gravel when I tried to stop too fast. Stupid greenhorn trick, that was, and I glanced at Cameron to see if he noticed.

He didn't seem to be paying any attention, so I put the Blazer in drive and headed out of there. I didn't drive too fast and I was careful not to do anything else to attract attention. The whole place looked emptier than a bum's billfold, but I still had that creepy feeling of being watched. You know how you can always tell when somebody's eyes are on you. It felt like that.

Maybe I was imagining things.

But then again, maybe not. We got to the gate where the camp ended and the dirt road began, and Cameron had to get out and open it. It was one of those big aluminum cattle gates and it wasn't locked, just held shut with a twist of yellow nylon rope to keep it from blowing open in the wind.

But anyway, *somebody* must have been watching us, because while Cameron was fumbling with the gate I heard a shout somewhere behind us. The game was up!

Cameron heard it too, and he didn't waste any more time trying to be quiet. He hauled off and kicked the gate open the rest of the way, then ran for the passenger side door.

He jumped in, and I spun gravel and sideswiped the gate on the way out. It hadn't finished opening all the way and I didn't have time to keep from hitting it. I heard metal screeching, and it left two or three long ugly scratches along the side of the Blazer.

"Go! Go!" Cameron yelled.

"I'm going!" I yelled right back.

To tell you the truth, I was terrified. Driving Justin's truck on back roads was slow and easy and he was always there to help me if I needed it. This was nothing like that. In fact, this was a nightmare. The pine trees were crowded close on both sides of the road, and there were deep ditches I was pretty sure I couldn't get out of if I slid into one. So I gripped the steering wheel tight in both hands and kept my eyes glued to the road, trying to keep from killing both of us.

Cameron didn't seem like he was worried about my driving, though. He had his window down and was looking behind us.

"Uh-oh. Here they come," he said. That was the last thing I wanted to hear, but there was nothing I could do about it right then except keep driving. I thought I was getting the hang of the Blazer by then, but learning how to drive while you're flying down a dirt road in the mountains with a pack of wolves hot on your tailpipe is not the easiest thing in the world to do. Try it yourself sometime if you don't believe me.

I had no idea where I was going, but the road snaked on through the woods with no turns or forks in sight, so I didn't have much chance to get lost. There were sometimes side roads that branched off, but they were all weedy and overgrown and I knew better than to turn off onto any of them. That wouldn't do anything but get us caught when we hit a dead end or a fallen log or a wash-out or anything else that blocked the way. If a road looks like nobody ever uses it, then that probably means it doesn't lead anywhere. I was also afraid of getting lost and driving in circles. The smartest thing to do was to keep on straight ahead.

I hoped.

The roads were dry as dust, and the Blazer kicked up so much dirt behind us that I guess it was choking the wolves to death. They dropped back a pretty good distance, so much that we even lost sight of them for a few minutes now and then around curves and over hills. That was good, sort of, even though I knew we'd never lose them that way. The dust cloud would always show them which way we went.

After a while we crested a little ridge and came to a T in the road that looked an awful lot like the one I saw yesterday when I was on foot. In fact I was ninety-nine percent sure it was the same one. If it was, then I needed to turn left to get to the highway.

I didn't have much time to think about it, but for some reason I turned right this time instead. I'm not sure why. The wolves were out of sight behind us, so maybe I was hoping they'd take the wrong fork when they came to that place. They had to know where the highway was, and they had to be pretty sure I knew. They'd probably guess that's where I was headed. The new road also had more gravel and less dirt than the one we just came from, so we wouldn't kick up near as much of a dust cloud as we had been. It was a slim hope, but it was better than none at all.

I turned too fast and the Blazer fishtailed on the gravel and I almost lost control and hit the ditch. I had to slam on the brakes and almost stop before I dared go on.

Cameron's eyes were big as dinner plates and my hands were shaking from the close call, but there was nothing we could do except to keep going.

I drove slower for a while, partly so we'd kick up less dust and partly to settle my nerves after that almost-wreck. The wolves never did catch up with us again after that, and I almost dared to hope we'd lost them by turning this way.

After what seemed like a long time we started passing houses once in a while. Then all of a sudden the road turned to pavement, and that was even better. No more dust trail or tire tracks to give us away to anybody who might be following us, and we could go faster, too.

Several miles later we came to a bridge, and just upstream I recognized the little beach where the people in the pickup truck had been parked yesterday afternoon when I floated by in that leaky tube. It seemed like a month ago.

I knew where I was, then. This was the Caddo River again, and all I needed to do was head south on the highway that ran beside it. So that's what I did, and within another ten minutes we were back in Glenwood.

At first it was hard for me to believe it had been that easy, but I wasn't dumb enough to think it was over yet. I was sure the wolves wouldn't give up that soon. They had to have another trick or two up their nasty little sleeves, and that's what worried me. Not knowing what might happen is always the hardest part of any bad situation, you know.

But the Blazer was running low on gas, and I didn't really have a driver's license anyway, and all we had was three bucks in change that Cameron found in the ashtray. That wouldn't be anywhere near enough to get back home, that's for sure. Not to mention the fact that we were driving a stolen car, sort of. I hoped it might get us another ten or twenty miles down the road so we'd be harder to find, but after that I didn't know what we'd do.

"We've got to ditch this car, dude," Cameron said.

"What, you mean like right now? How come? I think we lost them back there on the dirt road, at least for a while," I told him. He was already shaking his head before I even finished.

"Not for long we didn't. This is my mom's car. It's got OnStar and she'll find out exactly where we are as soon as she gets a chance to call them. She doesn't have cell service up in the mountains but she will as soon as she gets closer to town," he said.

I sighed. I knew it had been too easy. No wonder they hadn't followed us harder.

Cameron popped open the glove box and rooted around a few seconds until he pulled out a red mp3 player and a set of ear buds, then slipped them in his pocket.

"Might as well take this, you know. It's mine anyway," he said.

Just then the engine died. I guess Cameron's mom must have reached a place where her cell phone worked, and she called OnStar and had them kill the motor. It also meant she knew exactly where we were, and the wolves would be right on top of us in a matter of minutes.

The Blazer was still rolling, so I turned the wheel and managed to pull into a parking slot in front of the Diamond Bank. It was closed and we were the only car in the parking lot. Nobody could possibly overlook us if they drove by on the highway. I wished we could have found a place where we didn't stick out like a bug on a plate, but oh well. I tested the engine again just to make sure, and it was deader than road kill.

We were in a pretty tight spot, but in spite of everything I actually felt pretty cocky for pulling off my third great escape in two days. I remembered Laura calling me a slippery little fish back at the deer camp, and I wished I could have been there to see the look on her face when she found my room empty. I smiled a little, just imagining it. They didn't know who they were dealing with!

Yeah, I was really thinking stuff like that at the time, much as it embarrasses me to admit it now. I hope I'm not that full of myself all the time.

But busting out was one thing, and staying that way was a whole 'nother matter. So far I hadn't done too well at that half of the problem. That was enough to knock me back down to reality, when I thought about it.

We jumped out of the car, but instead of hightailing it away from there, Cameron yanked open the back door and started digging through the trash in the back seat.

"What are you doing, boy? We've got to get away from here!" I said.

"We've got to find the journal and the maps first. I know they're in here somewhere. I almost forgot about it, but we can't leave without them," he said.

He might as well have been speaking Greek for all I knew, but there was no time to ask questions or fight about it.

Sometimes you have to just trust people, you know. It's not always easy and you can't always have a reason for it. Cameron knew the danger as well as I did, so if there was something in the back seat so important that he was willing to risk getting caught just to find it, then I had to believe it was worth it, too. I opened the door on my side and started digging.

The Blazer was full of junk, and most of it was just trash. Nobody saves McDonald's bags for any good reason that I can think of. I wasn't sure exactly what I was supposed to be looking for, but I was pretty sure it wasn't burger wrappers.

I couldn't pay attention like I should have, because I kept wanting to look at the highway to see if anybody was slowing down. Nobody did, but I was antsy anyway. We probably had at least five minutes or so before the wolves could possibly get there, but you never knew for sure. I wanted to get gone.

I don't like piggy people who fill up their cars like trash cans. It makes it stink inside and it's just nasty. The Blazer was like that, and more than once I wanted to hold my nose while I dug through there. Somebody had left half a cheeseburger on the seat, and it had been there so long it was dried out like a piece of wood. I almost hurled when I came across that little jewel.

It seemed like it took forever, but really it couldn't have been more than a minute or so before I found a US

Geological Survey section map for southern Montgomery County with several spots marked on it in red ink and others in pencil. It looked like the red ones had been pencil to start with, and then marked over with a red pen later on. I couldn't make hide nor hair of what it was supposed to mean or why those particular spots were marked. They all looked like they were out in the middle of nowhere to me.

There were two other section maps rolled up with the first one, and they were marked with those same pencil scribbles in various places, but no red marks. I didn't take the time to look any closer.

I know how to read section maps because Justin uses them a lot when he has to go out and do field work. Oil wells don't always have nice neat addresses on streets, and sometimes you have to use topographical maps to find them instead. He used to take me with him now and then and he taught me how to read his maps so I could give him directions. I never really thought much about it before, but now I was glad I learned.

"Hey Cameron, is this what you're looking for?" I asked him, holding up the first section map.

"Yeah, that's it! We have to find the journal too, though," he said.

I folded up the maps and stuck them in my front pocket. They made a big bulky wad of paper, but it was still better than carrying them.

Right under the maps there was a school notebook with some writing in it that I didn't have time to read, but I grabbed that too without even asking Cameron if it was important.

Then I found what had to be the journal. It was a very old-looking book with crumbly pages which was shoved down there next to the rotten cheeseburger in the middle of the seat. It was bound in cracked brown leather, and it was partly burnt on one of the bottom corners. Cameron saw it at the same time I did and snatched it up.

Then he brushed aside some trash on the floorboard and grabbed a skateboard out from underneath it.

"Have you got anything *else* in there you want to take?" I asked, with just a touch of irritation.

"Nah, that's all, dude. It's just this was expensive and I didn't want to leave it. But let's get out of here," he said, slamming the back door.

I made sure to lock the doors before we left, and then I threw the keys into some thick azalea bushes in front of the bank. A storm drain would have been even better, but I didn't see one handy. The more time they wasted dealing with the Blazer, the better.

"Come *on*, dude. We don't have time for all that," Cameron said, looking out at the highway behind us. It couldn't have been more than five minutes since we parked the Blazer, but he was acting scared and I can't say I blamed him.

"All right, let's go," I agreed.

We took off at a fast run, getting behind the bank first and then crossing through some trees until we came to another street. I still didn't feel safe, so we kept going for quite a while, even ducking through back yards and alleys when we had to, to help stay out of sight. We got barked at by several dogs, but that was about it.

"Dang, this thing gets heavy after a while," Cameron said, setting his skateboard down on the pavement. We were walking down a narrow alley between two buildings where nobody was likely to see us, and it seemed like a good place to stop and rest. He was a little out of breath from running, but then so was I.

"Yeah, let's take a break for a few minutes. I think we're safe here," I said. He sat down on his board, and I found an old plastic milk crate to sit on. The alley was full of crud like that, so it wasn't hard to find something.

"So what now?" Cameron asked after a while.

"We need to find a phone so I can call my uncle. He'll come get us and then we can figure out what to do once we're safe away from here," I told him.

"You're sure he'd come?" Cameron asked.

"Yeah, I live with him. He wouldn't let me down," I said confidently.

"You must be Zach, then," he said. That's when I suddenly remembered I'd never actually told him who I was. There hadn't been time.

"Uh, yeah. That's me. How'd you know?" I asked.

"Aw, I've been around awhile. I hear things. I'm Cameron Parker, by the way," he said, sticking his hand out. I shook it because it would have been rude not to, but I couldn't help wondering about him anyway, now that I had time to think about it. His mother was the one who owned the Blazer, which meant she was either a *loup-garou* herself or else she was in cahoots with them some kind of way. So what did that mean about Cameron, then?

I think I would have had a hard time trusting him, except for one thing. I knew he'd been locked up at the deer camp, the same way I was. I'd seen the way Laura slapped him and I'd heard the way she talked to him. After all that, it was hard for me to believe he was just a mole-rat. And like

I said, sometimes you just have to trust people, even when it's hard.

Still, I couldn't help glancing at his fingernails just to make sure. He noticed, and held them up so I could see better. They were normal, just like mine.

"Nope, they never changed me yet," he said, half smiling. I was embarrassed that he caught me looking, but at least he seemed to think it was funny instead of getting mad at me.

"You seem like you know a lot of things," I finally said, lamely. I wasn't sure what else to say. Cameron just shrugged.

"I know what I know, that's all," he said. It was a cryptic thing to say, and I didn't feel like leaving it at that. In spite of what I said about trusting him, I had to know more.

"Then tell me what this is all about, if you can," I asked.

"That would be a long story, dude," he said.

"I've got nothing better to do than listen," I pointed out.

"Well. . . true 'nuff. I'm your third cousin, to start with. That's why I know some of the things I know. My grandpa and yours were brothers," he said matter-of-factly.

There didn't seem to be a lot I could say about that right then, but you can bet I tucked it away in the back of my mind to think about later.

"All right. I guess that explains how you got hooked up with the wolves and why you know some stuff about me. But why'd they have you locked up, and what do they want with *me*?" I asked. Those were the things I really wanted to hear about.

"Oh, I know what they want *you* for. They think you know where the Sweet Spring is," he said. That didn't do anything but confuse me even more.

"Laura said it was because they wanted me to become a *loup-garou* after all," I said.

"Well. . . maybe that too, but that's not the main reason. She was probably just telling you something she thought you'd believe until she decided how much to trust you. Laura's really good at messing with your head, you know. You can't trust anything she says," he said.

None of that surprised me. I already knew better than to believe anything Laura said. But I didn't care about that; I wanted to hear more about the Sweet Spring, whatever *that* was.

"Okay, so what's the Sweet Spring?" I asked, getting right to the point.

Cameron looked at me curiously for a few seconds.

"You really don't know, do you?" he finally said, shaking his head.

"Nope, I'm afraid not," I told him.

"Hmm. . . Well, I guess it *would* be hard to swallow all at once, if you didn't know anything," he said, half to himself, "But never mind. They've been trying to find that spring for years and years. I don't know exactly what it does, but it's important because there's a prophecy or something about it. They say one of the boys in the seventh generation is supposed to use it to break the curse. That's either me or you, and- " he said.

"Whoa, slow down a minute. Seventh generation of *what*? And *who* says all that?" I asked. I felt like the ground had opened up at my feet and left me standing on the edge of a deep ocean of weirdness.

"You don't even know about *that?*" he asked, like he couldn't believe it. It made me feel stupid, and I hate feeling that way.

"No, I guess I don't. Tell me," I said, trying to be polite. Cameron shrugged again in that way he does.

"All right, Zach. There's not really that much more to tell anyway. A long time ago, a man named Daniel Trewick figured out how to become the first *loup-garou*, or at least the first one in our family. I'm not real sure about that part. But *he* always said one of his great-great-great-great grandsons would either break the curse or renew it, whatever that means. That's seven generations. He also said the Curse-Breaker would have a mark on him so they'd know which boy it was," he said.

"What was the mark?" I whispered.

"Bright blue eyes, just like yours and mine," he said, with a laugh that didn't sound like he thought it was very funny.

"But that's stupid. Anybody could have blue eyes," I objected.

"*You* try telling them that. They won't listen, I promise you," he said.

"Anyway, there are only two of us who fit the bill, just me and you," he went on.

"How do you know all this?" I asked him for the second time. I'd never heard anything remotely like it in my life. I used to think my parents never told me anything when I was younger, but I never imagined how *much* they didn't tell me.

"Well, if you hadn't run away then you'd know at least that much yourself. That's something everybody in the family has to learn. You can read more about it in the journal sometime if you really want to," he said.

"Okay then, go on," I said.

"Anyway, they never could make up their minds which one of us it was. Everybody was already real suspicious of you and why you didn't want to be like everybody else, and then when you ran away that clinched it. They were all sure you must be the Curse-Breaker. It took the heat off me a little bit, and for a while they forgot about everything else except trying to find you and stop you from wrecking things. That's why they wouldn't give up till they had you. You did an awful good job of hiding, I have to say. We like to have never found you," he said.

"You helped them?" I accused.

"Well, yeah, I kinda had to, you know. They would have started looking at *me* funny again if I hadn't. Just because they were sure you were the one didn't mean they forgot I was a suspect, too," he pointed out.

"Well, yeah, I can see that. So what happened next?" I asked.

"Oh, I got careless, said some things I shouldn't have, did some things I was stupid to have done. Made them wonder. And then they finally did catch you and found out you didn't seem to have a clue what was up, so then they started getting all narrow-eyed and suspicious about *me* again. They couldn't decide which one of us it was, so they locked us both up just to make sure. They don't take chances about stuff like that, Zach," he said quietly.

I chewed on all that for a while. Cameron didn't seem like he wanted to add anything else to what he'd already said, but there was one more thing I had to know.

"So why'd you help me then?" I finally asked, just as quietly.

"Well, why'd you help *me*, when you didn't know who I was or why I was there? You took a chance on getting caught and maybe worse, just for me. I've had to live my whole life being looked at like I was a stray dog that might turn and bite somebody any minute, 'cause they all wondered if I was the Curse-Breaker. Even my mom looks at me that way. She thinks I don't see it, but I do. I'm tired of it, Zach. I just want to be normal for a while, if I can be, and you're the first person I can remember who ever treated me that way," he said.

I didn't know what to say to that. I knew exactly what he was talking about and how he felt. He felt rejected. He knew more about the reasons behind it than I ever did, but I guess that doesn't make it hurt any less. There's no reason good enough to excuse it, and nothing anybody can say to fill up that empty spot. I knew it all too well.

But I thought I understood him now.

So I didn't say anything, just clapped him on the right shoulder and left it at that. Sometimes you say the most when you say the least.

The full version of
Behind Blue Eyes
is available now at your favorite retailer.

If you liked The Last Werewolf Hunter,
You might also like

Tycho

An honest answer is like a kiss on the lips.
-Proverbs 24:26

Chapter One

Tuesday, January 22, 2154

I was at school the day the world fell apart, in Dr. Weiss's advanced genetics class, as a matter of fact.

Back in those days I'd never heard of the Orion Strain, the Moon was nothing but a light in the sky, and the worst problem I ever had to deal with was forgetting to turn in my chemistry homework. Mrs. McClendon used to be a real beast about late assignments.

I know the world can never go back to the way it was before, but sometimes I can't help wishing, you know.

I remember I was supposed to be comparing two different strains of mouse DNA that afternoon; deadly dull stuff, to be honest. So maybe it was just boredom that led me to set aside my genetics project and hack my way into the mainframe of the World Health Organization instead. Molecular genetics happens to be my special field of study, and that's one of the best places to visit if you like such things.

It was nothing but a whim; I wasn't looking for anything in particular. But we have a saying in science, about how the most interesting discoveries are almost always the accidental ones. It's called serendipity, and it ended up saving my life that day.

At any given time, the World Health Organization kept tabs on a dozen or more disease outbreaks in local areas around the world to make sure they didn't become an epidemic. Nothing unusual about that, and the one I chose to read about that afternoon was called the Orion Strain. I picked that one mostly because the file was classified, and it amused me to break through the security system and find out what they were being so secretive about. I certainly didn't think it would end up radically changing my life. But that's what I mean about serendipity; a little bit of whimsical curiosity can change *everything*.

The Orion Strain turned out to be a low level bacterium which had popped up for the first time in Calcutta, India, about a week earlier, and the only mildly interesting thing about it was the high death rate. So far at least, it seemed to have killed pretty much a hundred percent of the people who caught it, within no more than thirty-six hours after exposure. It was a viciously deadly bug, to be sure, but then of course there are a lot of viciously deadly bugs in the world and most of them never amount to anything much. It made me wonder why the file had been classified at all.

Then I saw what the reason was, and I gasped out loud without thinking, nearly dropping my pencil on the floor.

Dr. Weiss crumpled his *Tampa Tribune* for a second to frown at me, and I quickly made it look like I was totally absorbed in mouse DNA. But as soon as he went back to reading his article, I completely forgot about my genetics assignment.

Because it wasn't the deadliness of the Orion Strain that caused the blood to drain from my face and made me feel like a lump of ice had suddenly come to rest right in the pit of my stomach. It was the interspecies infection rate.

That may sound technical, but all it means is whether some other animal can catch a disease or not. Like pigs can sometimes catch human flu, for example. The scary thing about the Orion Strain was that it was highly contagious to any warm-blooded animal. Any bird or mammal, basically. There was no way you could ever contain something like that; a rat or a bird or some such thing would always slip through any barrier you tried to set up and they'd carry the infection elsewhere. There'd be no stopping it.

I quickly set up a simulation on my computer to analyze how fast the bacteria might spread, using the most conservative estimates. And that's when I *really* got scared.

"Drew, come look at this," I finally managed to croak. Drew Breyer was my lab partner and one of my few actual friends. He was fiddling with the electrophoresis unit at the moment, pretending to accomplish something useful. He was actually supposed to be helping me with the mouse analysis, but I didn't much care. Finishing the work myself was easier anyway.

Nevertheless, he was still technically my lab partner, so he yawned and then ambled over to my workstation to have a look.

"What is it?" he asked in a low voice, staring at the numbers on the screen.

"It's a statistical analysis of the progress of a bacterium called the Orion Strain on the Indian subcontinent over the past week. Infection rate compared to kill rate, speed of transmission, that kind of thing," I managed to say. That was good; focusing on data was an easy way to divert my mind from the terrible implications.

"And?" Drew asked, raising one eyebrow.

"Don't you see it?" I asked, astonished at his thick-headedness.

"See what, Tyke?" Drew asked, with a touch of irritation.

Oh, my name is Tycho, by the way, after Tycho Brahe the famous astronomer. Tyke, for short. Which I guess might have been cute when I was three years old, but it was definitely a liability at the John Brooke Academy for Math and Science. I hated the nickname, but I was so used to it that I barely noticed anymore.

But I digress.

Drew's question frustrated me, mostly because it meant I wasn't explaining myself very well. I must have been more rattled than I thought I was. I made an effort to calm down and be reasonably logical.

"Look here. I got these records from the World Health Organization in Geneva. This germ is spreading *fast*, and so far there's been a kill rate of a hundred percent. Everybody that catches it dies," I explained.

"Yeah, I know how to read stats, Tyke," Drew said dryly.

"You're not the least bit worried about that?" I asked.

"About what? A nasty little disease in Calcutta? Why should I be worried about that? There are nasty new diseases all the time and they never amount to anything. They kill some people and then they disappear, which is exactly what this one will do. The very fact that it's so deadly only means it'll flame out sooner, because it'll kill all the available hosts. It says right here that they've already sealed off the city to keep it from spreading. Even if they don't find a cure, it'll be over in a week. Worse comes to worst, it'll wipe out Calcutta, maybe even a few other cities if they're sloppy about their quarantine. Bad, yes, but it's not like it's the whole world or anything," he said.

"No, Drew. Look here," I said, pointing at the section that dealt with interspecies crossovers. This time he didn't need to ask me what the numbers meant. He drew in his breath sharply, just like I had.

"Are you sure those numbers are right?" he asked, actually looking worried for the first time.

"Yeah, I'm sure. The interspecies crossover rate is *also* close to a hundred percent among birds and mammals. They can't close borders against birds and mice, now can they? And besides that, look here; it says the bacterium can also form spores which are estimated to survive in the environment for at least twenty years," I said.

Drew looked ill, and I could hardly blame him. If that data was correct, then we were staring at the end of the world.

"Where'd you get this?" he asked.

"I told you, I got it from the World Health Organization. I hacked their computer," I said, allowing myself a touch of pride in spite of everything. The administration of the Academy would have had a hissy fit if they'd known I was using school computers for hacking into government databases, but in the meantime what they didn't know wouldn't hurt them.

"But surely they'll find a vaccine, or some kind of treatment," he objected.

"Drew, you're not thinking. It'll be a week till the first wave of infections gets *here*. Maybe even less than that if a bird flies in from one of the affected areas. In ten days, at most, everybody in Tampa will be dead. I give it two weeks for the whole world, and that's being generous. That's not enough time to find a cure for anything. You should know that," I reminded him. Drew was a medical science student; he of all people ought to know how long it took to find treatments for disease.

"But there's always a chance," he insisted.

"Yeah, I guess there's always a chance, but I wouldn't bet on it," I said.

Drew was silent, thinking. He might be a slacker when it came to assignments, but he was still one of the most brilliant kids in the state of Florida; he could analyze the situation as well as anybody, and I watched as despair slowly clouded his eyes. Even if we told the administrators and even if they believed us, there was absolutely nothing to be done about it.

"You don't think there's anywhere we could go to ride it out?" he asked hopefully. I considered it, and then shook my head.

"No. There're nowhere in the world that birds don't go, not even the most remote islands you can think of. We'd have to find somewhere sealed up *tight* if we wanted to hide out, with enough food and supplies to last us twenty years or more. There's no place on Earth like that, unless it was already built and ready by now," I said dejectedly.

"So you're saying unless somebody miraculously finds a cure sometime in the next week or so, then we're toast. Is that it?" he asked.

"Yeah, that's pretty much it," I admitted.

"I can't believe there's nothing we can do," he insisted.

"I'm open to suggestions," I said.

There was silence for a long time, and then I could have sworn I saw the glint of a smile on Drew's face.

"There's no place on Earth we'd be safe, huh?" he asked, and then I was sure of it. Drew was actually *excited.*

"Nope, none at all. Maybe somewhere out in the middle of the ice cap in Antarctica where no animals ever go. But we don't have time or money to build a fortress out there and stock it with supplies," I agreed.

"What about somewhere else besides Earth, then?" Drew suggested. My first impulse was to call him an idiot, but then I reconsidered.

"You mean the space stations?" I asked.

"No, there's no way they'll last twenty years without fresh supplies from Earth. They'll run out of food, and spare parts, and things like that. Not a good option," he said.

"What are you talking about, then?" I asked.

"The Moon, buddy, the Moon!" he cried excitedly. In fact he let his voice rise just a little too high, and Dr. Weiss frowned at us again from behind his newspaper. Both of us were quick to take a sudden fascination with the numbers on my computer, and after a few seconds Dr. Weiss went back to ignoring us.

I chewed on my lip, thinking. I didn't know all that much about the Moon, but I remembered it had always been one of Drew's pet hobbies. His grandfather had been a member of the original survey team for the Lunar Terraform Project, fifty years ago or more, but he'd been killed in a storm that destroyed the research compound where he was working. Barnaby Station, if I remembered right. If I'd heard that story once, I'd heard it a million times.

Anyway, the idea hadn't worked out quite the way they'd planned, for some reason. All I could remember was that they'd wasted huge sums of money and then ended up never finishing the Project anyway. The only interesting thing about the whole boondoggle was a couple of footnotes in our genetics textbooks about *Macrocystis tranquilitatis,* a type of kelp, and *Makaira caeruleus,* a variety of blue marlin, both of which had been developed for the lunar environment right there at the Academy. I remembered vaguely that there was no salt in the seas of the Moon, so saltwater organisms had had to be modified to live in fresh water. I couldn't remember much else.

"I didn't think people could survive up there," I said skeptically, and Drew wrinkled his nose.

"Well. . . yes and no," he said.

"What's that supposed to mean?" I asked.

"It means there's breathable air, and drinkable water, and a somewhat functioning ecosystem. It's survivable," he said.

"I hear a 'but' in there somewhere," I said.

"*But.* . . it gets up to about 140 degrees during the day, minus 20 at night, there are incredible storms all the time, the radiation level is fairly high, and there's not much to eat," he said.

"I see. So instead of the Orion Strain, it's better to die from starvation, or heat stroke, or freezing to death, or maybe cancer? Not to mention the fact that we don't have a way to get there in the first place," I scoffed.

"There's still the old research compound at Lakeside Station. It's probably run down and ragged out after all this time sitting there empty, but we could knock it back into shape, I'm sure. It'll have heat and air conditioning, probably a hydroponics lab to grow food, maybe some radiation shielding. It's a *chance,* anyway. Better than sitting here twiddling our thumbs and then dying from the Orion Strain next week, don't you think?" Drew said.

I couldn't very well argue with that assessment, so I shifted my defense. Truthfully, I was desperate for Drew to convince me. When you're staring death in the face, you'll give just about anything for a plan that offers even the barest scrap of hope. Even an utterly stupid one like running off to the Moon.

"Doesn't matter anyway, since there's no way for us to get there," I reminded him.

"I'll have to think about that one," Drew finally admitted.

"Yeah, well. . . we got precious little time to think about it, buddy boy," I said.

"Yeah, I know. I'll talk to some people, see what we can come up with," he said.

"I'd be careful who I said anything to," I warned.

"Oh, come on, Tyke; give me a little credit. I know who's trustworthy and who's not," he said, shaking his head.

I shrugged and started to say something else, but just then the bell rang and I had to sign out of my workstation before the next class came in. There was no way I wanted anybody to see what I'd been working on.

I was preoccupied for the rest of the day and paid no attention to my classes. There didn't seem to be any point, when you thought about it. Biochemistry was interesting, sure, but two weeks from now what difference would it make to anybody?

After school was over at three, I didn't have the heart to get involved with any of the extracurricular things which the school offered, or even to go to the library like I usually did. I just trudged slowly back to the dorm room to lie down on my bed and stare blankly at the ceiling. The Academy was a residential school, and except during holidays all students lived on campus unless our families were close enough to drive us every day.

My parents passed away a long time ago, in a boating accident on Tampa Bay when I was four years old. I don't really remember very much about them, honestly. My dad was an astronomer and my mother was a math professor, and I know they named me Tycho because they hoped I'd grow up to become a famous scientist someday. I'm not sure if biology was exactly what they had in mind, but that's what I've always loved.

Anyway, ever since they died I've lived with my aunt and uncle, Joan and Philip Carpenter, and my four cousins out in Clearwater Beach. Their names were Chris, Jesse, Callum, and Veronica, and it so happened that Jesse and I were born just two weeks apart. We'd been best friends ever since preschool, and one of the things I'd always liked about the Academy was that I got to share a room with him.

People were always a little surprised that we both went to school together; the Academy isn't such an easy place to get into. You have to score really high on your placement exams in eighth grade, and then you have to apply and have an interview and all kinds of things. It's a very prestigious place, and by the time we graduate high school we'll already have a Master's degree in our chosen field. There were a lot of programs to choose from, some of them better than others, of course. The advanced genetics program was one of the very best, along with marine science and aerospace engineering. Those were our top three programs, and sometimes it humbled me to think I was a part of one of them. There have been a lot of famous people who went to this place, and a lot of famous teachers, too. Dr. Weiss had a Nobel prize for his work in genetics, and he was far from the only one.

Jesse and I had shared the same room for two and a half years, ever since we started ninth grade, and all that time together had made us tighter than ever.

That's why in spite of what I said to Drew about being careful who he talked to, I'd already decided to tell Jesse everything.

He came in about four-thirty, covered in sweat from running. He always ran five miles around the dirt track after school every day, rain or shine, hot or cold. It was unusually warm for January, and he flopped down on his bed with a sigh of contentment wearing nothing but his running shorts.

"A thousand blessings on the head of whoever invented air-conditioning!" he said with a theatrical flourish to no one in particular, and I couldn't help smiling a little. Jesse is nearly impossible not to like.

"I think that was Charles Carrier," I told him, sitting up and leaning my back against the cinderblock wall.

"Well, then, a thousand blessings on the head of Saint Charles Carrier!" Jesse said, grinning.

"Whatever, dude," I said, rolling my eyes.

"You'd say the same thing if you knew how warm it was out there today. Track was so hot I bet you could fry an egg on the dirt," Jesse said.

"Nobody put a gun to your head and forced you to go out there running today, Jesse," I pointed out.

"True, but I wouldn't want to get all weak and pale and flabby like some people I could mention, now would I?" he said, laughing. I shook my head at the good-natured dig; Jesse was always trying to get me to run or swim or get involved in some kind of athletic activity. I wouldn't go so far as to call myself weak and pale and flabby, but sometimes I did envy Jesse a little bit for his chiseled muscles and his careless good looks. He's big and tall and blond, like my Uncle Philip, and I'm small and dark-haired like my mother and Aunt Joan. No one who saw us together would ever have guessed we were related at all. He also loves athletics, and sports just aren't my thing, not by a long shot. I'm a pretty good swimmer, but that's about as far as it goes.

I was about to say so when there came a knock on the door. I got up to answer it and saw that it was Drew.

"Hey, Drew Dog, what's up?" Jesse called from the bed.

"Um. . . just need to talk to Tyke for a minute, that's all," he said.

"I'm guessing that means you want me to trot off and leave y'all alone, huh?" he asked, smiling.

That was another thing about Jesse; he's always enjoyed playing the redneck country boy role, ever since I can remember. We have a saying in Florida, that the farther north you go, the more South you get. It's nothing unusual to hear a drawly voice around Tampa, but Jesse definitely plays it up to the fullest.

"Well, yeah, it's kinda private. Sorry, Jesse," Drew said.

"Oh, it's okay. I needed to hit the showers before suppertime, anyway. I'll see y'all in a little while," Jesse said. He took a minute to gather up some clothes and a towel, and then headed down the hall toward the bathroom, whistling.

Chapter Two

Drew came inside to sit down on my bed, and I went back to leaning against the wall.

"What's up?" I asked, as soon as the door was shut.

"I think I found a way to get there, man," he said eagerly, eyes shining.

"Are you still hung up on that stupid moon idea?" I asked, and Drew looked a little hurt.

"Yeah, I am. And you ought to be, too, if you care about saving your own sorry hide," he said. I sighed.

"Sorry. . . I'm just stressed out to the max, I guess," I apologized.

"Well, yeah, no doubt. But listen. Like I said, I think I found a way to get us there," he repeated.

"I'm all ears," I said.

"Okay, so I was talking to Dr. Weiss this afternoon, and-" he began, and my jaw dropped.

"You told Dr. Weiss!" I exclaimed, horrified.

"No, no, I just had a hypothetical discussion with him, that's all.   I didn't really tell him anything," Drew explained hastily.

"Okay, go on, then," I said.

"He told me about one of the new space planes they're working on out at MacDill, the XR-339's. His wife works out there with my dad, you know," he said.

"Yeah, I know. What about it?" I asked.

"Okay, well, he said the XR-339 could take off from a runway just like a plane and enter low-Earth orbit without needing any rocket boosters. It's got a thorium-228 nuclear reactor for power instead and it's got a good enough range to reach the space stations and make it back.   They've tested it several times and it's come through with flying colors," Drew explained.

"And?" I asked.

"So then I went home and asked my dad about it, and he told me pretty much the same thing. He said a trip to the moon was a lot farther than it was rated for, but he couldn't think of any reason why it wouldn't make it," Drew explained, smugly.

"I'm surprised they told you all that," I asked, skeptically.

"It's not like it's classified information or anything, Tyke. They've had XR's forever. They used to have old clunky ones even back when the Terraform Project was still going on.   It's just that nobody uses them anymore because rockets are so much safer and cheaper. That's what Dad and Mrs. Weiss are working on; trying to build an XR plane which is safe and cost-competitive," he said.

For the first time, I started to feel the first twinges of hope.

"Are they hard to fly?" I asked guardedly.

"Nope, not at all. Anybody who knows how to pilot a plane can fly one, no sweat," Drew said.

"Yeah, but I bet they guard that place like Fort Knox, Drew. We'd never get in there to *see* one of those planes, much less leave with one," I pointed out.

"Most people, yeah, that's probably true. But we got *connections*, buddy. Peggy Weiss can get in there any time she wants to, and so can my dad. They could slip the rest of us in there, and then we can pinch that ship like taking candy from a baby. No sweat," Drew explained.

"Maybe," I said, doubtfully.

"I'm telling you, it'll work. We just have to convince my dad and the Weisses, that's all. That's where you come in, Tyke. You're the one who hacked that computer and got the data. You'll have to explain everything to my dad first, and then he can help with the Weisses; they've been friends forever. Then we're good to go!" Drew said confidently.

"How many people are we talking about taking along on this trip?" I asked. I still couldn't believe I was letting myself get sucked into his whole crazy Moon scheme, although I had to admit I couldn't think of anything else to try. When there's only one option on the table, then all you can do is go along with it. No matter how crazy it is.

"Dad said they've got thirty-one seats, and that's including the pilot and copilot chairs," he said soberly.

"So we can only take thirty-one people?" I asked.

"That's about the size of it," he agreed reluctantly.

That bothered me.   How do you pick just thirty-one people and offer them a slim-but-real chance to survive a catastrophe, and then leave the rest behind?   That's a hard choice to have to make.

I didn't want to think about it right then, so I changed the subject.

"Have you talked to anybody except Dr. Weiss and your dad?" I asked.

"I talked to Tabby and Aron, that's all," he said, and I nodded. Tabby was his sister and Aron was his best friend, so I would have expected those two, at least.

"Nobody else? They won't talk to anybody, will they?" I asked.

"Nope. I told them to keep their mouths shut. Aron's got no friends to tell, anyway, and Tab wouldn't talk if I told her not to," he said.

I thought about that.

"I have to tell Jesse, though," I said abruptly.

"Well. . . whatever you think. Anyway, I told Mom I invited you over for supper tonight at seven o'clock. I didn't tell her why, but that's your chance to convince Dad, so you better have all your ducks in a row. Me and Tab will do our best to help you out, but this'll mostly be your thing, Tyke," he said.

"Gee, thanks," I murmured, and Drew sighed.

"It was the best I could do, buddy. You know that, right?" he asked earnestly, and I nodded.

"I know, Drew. I'm sorry. I'll be there at six-thirty and then we'll see what happens," I said.

"All right, see you then!" he said, and a few minutes later he was gone.

It was already almost five, so I went to one of the computer labs in the dormitory and signed on. It took me almost forty-five minutes to download my data and organize it in such a way that it looked respectable, and then I took a few minutes to shave and comb my hair. Drew's parents had seen me often enough that I knew they wouldn't be impressed just because I gussied up before I came to supper, but I was nervous and it helped me calm down a little bit.

Drew lived about six or seven blocks from the Academy, in a little brown bungalow down by the river. There were a couple of sickly-looking palm trees in the front yard and it was nothing special as far as houses go, but I think they stayed there mostly so Drew and Tabby could live at home while they went to high school. As soon as those two graduated, I was pretty sure the Breyers would move out to Citrus Park or Treasure Island or one of the other nicer suburbs. I'd heard them mention it a time or two.

There was a sea breeze blowing in off the Gulf, and it was cool enough by then that I didn't mind the walk. Drew and Tabby were sitting on the front deck when I showed up, and I waved to them. Drew waved back, and Tabby, as usual, did not. She seemed to live with a permanent grudge against the whole world in general and other human beings in particular, and she was close to the most unlikable individual I'd ever met in my life. Her only redeeming features were that she adored Drew and she was incredibly smart. She was the only girl in the aerospace engineering program at the Academy, and she well deserved her spot.

She said nothing as I climbed the steps, even while Drew clapped me on the back and ushered me into the house.

Mr. Breyer was sitting in the living room watching the news, and Mrs. Breyer was in the kitchen cooking. It smelled like meatloaf, which was just fine with me. They both said hi when we entered the house.

"When do you think I should talk to him?" I whispered.

"Wait till after supper; that's always the best time to tell him anything," Drew whispered back.

So in the meantime we sat down at the kitchen table and chatted about school and computers and unimportant things, with Mr. and Mrs. Breyer throwing in a comment or two now and then when they weren't too involved with the cooking or the news. I enjoyed myself, just like I always did; that house had always felt like a second home to me, almost since the first day I came to the Academy. Besides Jesse, Drew was my best friend.

The meatloaf was tender and delicious when we finally got to eat, and even the salad was good. I always liked to say that I hated rabbit food, but Gina Breyer could whip up a salad even I enjoyed.

But all good things end eventually, and after the plates were loaded into the dishwasher and the five of us were sitting together in the living room, I knew the moment of truth had come. I waited for a commercial break, and then cleared my throat.

"Um, Mr. Breyer, there was something I wanted to talk to you about, if you've got a little time," I said.

"Sure, sport. What's on your mind?" he asked, glancing at me.

"I guess you heard about what's been going on in India, right?" I began carefully. I didn't really think he would have heard anything yet, but it seemed like a good way to break the ice.

"No, can't say that I have. What do you mean?" he asked.

"I heard about a new kind of bacteria this morning, over there in Calcutta. It's called the Orion Strain," I said.

"Really?" he asked, like he wasn't too interested. I needed to get his undivided attention, so I decided this was no time to be delicate.

"The reason I mention it is because I think that bacteria is about to wipe out the whole human race," I said bluntly.

"Surely that's a bit much, don't you think?" he said, laughing a little.

"No, sir, I really don't think it is. In fact, I know it's not. I hacked into the World Health Organization computers today and found out all about it. I've got the data right here," I said, pulling out my papers.

Mr. Breyer furrowed his brow and clicked off the TV with his remote. He knew me well enough to know that I could certainly have hacked into a government computer if I'd wanted to. Any other time he might have lectured me about how irresponsible it was to break into other people's databases and so forth, but not that night.

"I see," he said.

"So far, it's been a hundred percent fatal, and not just to humans, either. It's deadly to all birds and mammals, too. So far the only cases have been in Calcutta, but I ran an analysis this morning and it'll spread exponentially. If nothing changes, then it'll be here in Tampa no later than a week from now, and all over the world within two weeks. I don't think we can stop it," I said neutrally, doing my very best to stay calm and reasonable. If you get upset then people stop listening, and I desperately needed him to believe me.

"I've looked at the data myself, Dad; I think he's right," Drew chimed in.

"Can I see that booklet, please?" Mr. Breyer asked expressionlessly, and I wordlessly handed him the data I'd printed earlier.

"Come here, honey; help me look at this," he said to his wife, and she moved closer beside him so she could see. She was a social director at one of the ritzy retirement communities in Citrus Park, so I'm not sure why he thought she'd know much about biology or even statistics, but I didn't say a word. Both of them read the papers silently, and I watched them grow pale as they grasped the significance.

"Have you told anyone else about this?" he asked suddenly, looking back and forth between me and Drew.

"No, just Tabby," Drew said, and I shook my head.

"Have *you* told anybody, Tab?" Mr. Breyer asked, looking at his daughter.

"No, Dad," she said.

Mr. Breyer rubbed his temples and thought hard.

"This is pretty serious stuff, kids. I won't lie to you; I hope you're wrong. I hope we all missed something, because if not. . . " he shook his head, leaving the rest unspoken. We all knew what he meant.

"We should ask Rob and Peggy about this," Gina said, referring to Dr. Weiss and his wife. That was exactly what

I'd hoped one of them would say, because if we were to have any chance at all of getting ourselves a ticket to the Moon, then we'd have to get Peggy Weiss on our side first.

She went to the phone to call them, and after a hurried conversation the Weisses agreed to come over. In the meantime, Mr. Breyer kept on rubbing his temples and thinking.

"If this is true, then there's nothing we can do. *Nothing.* We might as well quit our jobs and enjoy the time we've got left," he said after a while. It sounded like the ideal time to mention the escape plan, and I glanced meaningfully at Drew.

"Dad, we did think of one possible solution," he said, and Jason Breyer looked at his son.

"What is it, Drew?" he asked, as if his mind were a thousand miles away.

"We could always go to the Moon," Drew said.

For a second, it was almost like the idea didn't register in Mr. Breyer's mind, but when it did he smiled.

"You mean the XR-339. That's why you asked me if it could make it to the Moon earlier!" he cried.

"And you said yes, it probably could," Drew reminded him, smiling himself. Mr. Breyer must have been almost as much of a Moon fanatic as his son, because he didn't ask any questions about whether or not we could survive up there for twenty years or what the conditions might be like or anything else like that. And of course, I'm sure he already knew all there was to know about the XR-339 and what it might be capable of. He had the kind of look on his face that a man gets when he's just won a million dollar lottery.

Then his smile faded.

"There are only thirty-one seats on that plane, Drew. That's enough for me and you and Mom and Tab, and Tycho, and the Weisses and their two kids, maybe a few other people. What happens to everybody else?" he asked.

It was the same question I'd been thinking about earlier, and there was no good answer for it, of course. Then Tabby spoke up.

"Dad, you always told us we should do everything we can for humanity, didn't you?" she said gruffly.

"Yes, Tab, and that's exactly what concerns me right now; escaping to safety ourselves and abandoning all these other people to die," he said.

"Would it save them, if we stayed behind?" she asked.

"No," he admitted.

"Can we take them with us?" she asked.

"No," he said.

"Then we haven't done them any harm, by trying to save ourselves if we can," she pointed out. It sounded harsh, but there was no way we could argue with her.

"But how do we *choose* who to save and who to leave behind, Tab? That's what worries me," he said.

I never got to hear Tabby's answer to that, because just then Dr. and Mrs. Weiss arrived, with Johnny and Bethany in tow. Neither of them were students at the Academy, so I didn't know them all that well even though we were all roughly the same age. I knew Johnny went to school at the music conservatory downtown because I'd heard Drew mention it before, but I wasn't sure about Bethany.

I was braced to have a tough time convincing Dr. Weiss of anything because I knew how demanding he could be in class. The way he grilled his students over every tiny step in their research was legendary. You never made a careless statement in front of that man unless you were prepared to back it up, that was for sure. It made my palms sweaty just remembering some of the sessions I'd endured with him.

But surprisingly, it didn't take all that long to convince him. He just read the data report and listened to Drew's idea, and then immediately started making plans to put it into effect. Maybe it helped that he was such a brilliant and logical man; he could read the data and figure out instantly what had to be done, without the slightest hesitation. Most people in a situation like that would have been tempted to sit back and take a wait-and-see attitude about things, to find out whether the threat was real or not before they acted. But there are occasions when waiting too long to take action will get you killed, and Dr. Weiss was smart enough to see the writing on the wall while there was still time.

Peggy Weiss agreed that she and Mr. Breyer could probably find a way to smuggle a group of people into the hangar where the XR-339 was kept, and then come up with some excuse to get us inside the plane. She could fly it, once they managed that.

They were busily hashing out all the details when Mr. Breyer finally broached the delicate subject of who should be taken along. But Dr. Weiss had an immediate answer for that, too.

"We have to take people who can repopulate the human race. We need as many healthy young people as we can find; hopefully some intelligent ones," he declared, and Peggy Weiss quickly nodded her agreement.

That seemed like a distasteful way of choosing people, at least to my way of thinking. I like to think I'm worth something besides just breeding stock. If that's all human beings were good for, then why bother to preserve the human race at all?

But I kept my thoughts to myself and said nothing. Dr. Weiss wouldn't have listened to me, anyway.

After several hours of discussion, it was decided that the best source of people to take would be students from the Academy, if we could find any, and that me and Drew and Tabby should discreetly approach some of our friends to get a feel for who might be willing and able to join such a desperate mission for survival.

I honestly couldn't think of anyone at school that I liked and trusted enough to ask, other than Jesse. Drew had already talked to Aron, and maybe those two would be able to think of more. Dr. Weiss also insisted that there had to be equal numbers of boys and girls; more of his breeding regimen, I guess.

It was agreed that we'd all keep in touch and that all potential recruits would have to be personally approved by Dr. Weiss. I didn't like that part of the plan, either, but since he·was the one with the keys to the ship, I didn't have a lot of say-so. We also agreed that if all went well, we'd try to launch the ship no later than the day after tomorrow. Time was running short.

Chapter Three

I walked home that night by myself, even though Mr. Breyer offered to drive me. I needed time to think, and I wanted to be alone for that. Two days wasn't much time to find the right people and convince them to go. I still didn't like Dr. Weiss's attitude about who should be chosen and why, but like I said there wasn't an awful lot I could do about it.

Jesse was reading when I got back to the dorm room, and I shut the door quietly behind me and locked it for the night before stripping down to my shorts and t-shirt to lie down.

"Jesse?" I asked.

"Yeah, what is it, Tyke?" he asked absently, still absorbed in his book. I glanced at the cover and saw that it was a history of space flight. Jesse had always wanted to lead the first mission to Mars someday, if such a thing ever ended up happening. I think that's why he decided to study aerospace avionics at the Academy, even though he was smart enough that he could have gone into the engineering division with Tabby if he'd wanted to. Avionics wasn't good for much of anything nowadays unless you wanted to fly back and forth to the space stations, but Jesse's head was full of dreams about leading a voyage of exploration to the far ends of the solar system. Most of the governments in the world had written off space exploration a long time ago as too expensive and not worth the investment, but I guess a boy can always dream.

"If you knew the world was about to end next week, what would you do?" I asked.

"Make sure I ate all the greasy food I wanted and never run track again," he joked, and then furrowed his brow when he glanced at my face. He put a marker in his book and laid it aside, and then leaned on his elbow to look at me straight.

"You're really serious, huh?" he finally asked.

"Yeah, I kinda am," I nodded.

"Then I think I'd go home and spend whatever time was left with the people I loved, and then whenever the end came I'd be okay with that," he said seriously.

"Really?" I asked.

"Yeah, really. I'd wake up in a better place, anyway," he said, absently touching the gold cross around his neck. It had been a present from Aunt Joan three months ago when he turned sixteen, and as far as I knew he'd never taken it off ever since.

"But what if you had a chance to get away and live?" I pressed.

"Tyke, I get the feeling you're not talking about maybes, here. What's up?" he asked.

So I told him everything, and when I asked him to go along he didn't laugh.

"What about Mom and Dad, and Chris and Callum and Veronica?" he asked soberly.

"I don't know. It's up to Dr. Weiss who gets to come and who doesn't," I admitted.

"Then ask him. If they can't go then I think I'd rather stay here and take my chances," he said quietly. He was right, and I was ashamed of myself for ever thinking otherwise. I quickly made up my mind that if Jesse and the others couldn't go, then I wouldn't go, either.

"Well, he said he wanted young people. Chris is eighteen, Veronica is twelve, and Callum is nine, so maybe he'll be all right with them, at least. He says we have to take people who can have a lot of kids and keep the human race alive," I said lightly, and Jesse did laugh then.

"No way. Seriously?" he asked.

"Yeah, seriously," I said.

"Well, Chris never said whether he wanted ten kids or not, and I doubt if Callum and Veronica have ever even thought about it yet, but hey, whatever the good doctor thinks. I'm willing to do stud duty if they want me to," he said, and then *I* had to laugh.

"I'm pretty sure he's serious, Jesse," I said.

"Yeah, well, Dr. Weiss has always been a stick-in-the-mud anyway. But if all he cares about is babies, then what about Mom and Dad? Dad's thirty-seven and Mom's. . . what? Thirty-five, I think? I guess they could still have a few more if it came to that, but I'm pretty sure they didn't really plan on it," he said.

"I don't know; I can ask," I said.

"Do that," Jesse said.

"Do you think they'll come?" I asked.

"Yeah, I'm pretty sure they would, under the circumstances. We need to talk to them, though," he said absently, as if lost in thought.

"No doubt," I agreed.

"Who else is going, so far?" he asked.

"Drew and Tabby, Johnny and Bethany Weiss, Aron Anderson, Mr. and Mrs. Breyer, Dr. and Mrs. Weiss, and I think that's all so far. Hopefully you and me and the others," I said.

"Well. . . I'm pretty sure Chris will want to bring his girlfriend, and *she* probably wouldn't come unless her sister and her parents had a spot. And then I thought about asking Leah, and I'm sure she'll want her brother and her mom to come. The spots are gonna fill up fast at that rate, Tyke," he said. Leah was Jesse's girlfriend.

I was thinking the same thing, and added up the numbers in my head as fast as I could. That added thirteen people to the list just by asking Jesse, if all those other people agreed to come and Dr. Weiss agreed to let them.

The list was indeed filling up fast.

Me and Jesse skipped school the next morning and rode the bus out to Clearwater Beach. It's about an hour's ride, on a good day. But we needed to talk to everybody, and there was no time to waste. I'd called Dr. Weiss the night before and he'd agreed that the Carpenters could come, and all the others Jesse had suggested, but it was up to us to convince them. I'm not sure he would have been quite so generous if time hadn't been so short, but as it was he probably thought as long as the people were young and healthy then that was the best he could hope for.

Aunt Joan was in the laundry room when we got there, and Uncle Philip was at work, of course. Chris was with him, and the other two were at school. There wouldn't be a chance to talk to anybody for a few hours, at least.

"Boys, what are you doing out of school?" Aunt Joan called as soon as she saw us come in. She was a small, slight woman with dark hair, green eyes, and a ready smile. Everybody said she looked just like my mother, but then of course they'd been sisters.

"Dr. Weiss gave us an assignment today," Jesse said cryptically, which was completely true without saying too much just yet.

"Oh, I see. Well you better get on with it, then," she said, giving both of us a kiss before she went back to finishing her laundry. I wanted to tell her not to waste her time washing clothes, but I didn't. It was better to let her have a few more hours of untroubled happiness before her world got turned completely upside down. She was a nurse at one of the hospitals in Saint Petersburg, but on her off days she liked to work around the house. She was like a hummingbird, always full of energy and always doing something. The lady literally couldn't sit still for longer than five minutes. She'd always been that way, ever since I could remember.

Me and Jesse had already packed our bags, so there was no need to do any of that. Dr. Weiss had said everybody could take whatever would fit in one large-sized backpack, and that was all. He'd insisted that it had to be a backpack, too, so nothing would look suspicious when we got to the plane the next day. I'd taken some clothes, and a few pictures, and few other odds and ends. Jesse took an extra pair of running shoes and a wooden music box that his grandmother had given him a long time ago. Neither one of us had much that we couldn't do without.

But we still had several hours before Philip and Chris got home, and neither of us wanted to sit at the house all day.

"Come on, Tyke; let's go somewhere," Jesse said, and I nodded.

We lived on Papaya Street, which is close to the center of Clearwater Beach. The house wasn't right on the waterfront because we couldn't afford anything that pricey, but it was close enough to make no never mind. You could walk three blocks one way to the beach, or three blocks the other way to the marina.

I was sure Jesse was headed for one or the other of those two places, but I didn't know which one until we got out to the sidewalk. It turned out to be the marina.

Jesse has a Hobie catamaran, not too big but pretty darned fast when the wind is up, and I guess he wanted to sail her one last time while we still could.

We unhitched from the dock and Jesse slowly took her out into the Gulf. He turned north to follow the coast without saying much, skimming along the water in the light breeze. There were a few little islands up that way with no development on them, just white sand dunes and beach grass. Places like that are hard to find in Florida; pretty much every beach in the state seems to have its own resort hotel or housing development nowadays. But there are still a few wild ones, if you know where to look. Jesse beached us on one of them a few miles from town, and we had lunch on top of the dunes.

"I'm gonna miss this," he murmured, gazing out over the crystal blue waters of the Gulf. For all you could tell, we might have been the only human beings for a thousand miles.

"Yeah, me too," I agreed, running some of the sand through my fingers. There might be beaches on the Moon, but I doubted they'd look like the ones in Florida.

Before long the ants found my Coke, and I choked and sprayed when I accidentally drank a few of them.

"And so the bugs inherit the earth after all," I said in disgust, pouring out the rest of my Coke on the sand, along with all the ants in the can. Jesse edged away and I remembered how much he hated bugs and spiders. It was his one and only semi-phobia, and normally I would have teased him about it mercilessly, but I wasn't in the mood for it that day.

"Don't worry, I'll cover it up," I said, and brushed sand over the wet spot so it wouldn't attract any other critters.

"Thanks. I just can't stand bugs, that's all," he apologized.

"I know; don't mention it," I said.

We finished our lunch in peace and then swam in the waves for a little while before Jesse took us back out, this time way out across the water so far that we couldn't see land at all.

"You're sure we couldn't just find some island a long way off in the middle of the ocean and live there for a while?" he asked presently, but I had to shake my head.

"There's nowhere far enough. The birds would find us, or the seals, or the dolphins, or something like that. I already thought about all that, bro," I told him.

"Yeah, I know. I thought about it, too. Just thought I'd ask," he sighed, and then turned his attention back to the sails. It was getting close to the time school should have been out, so he turned us around and took us back to the marina, where he neatly put the boat back in its slip.

"Sorry if I'm bummed; I just needed that," he said on the way home, and I nodded.

Callum and Veronica were out of school by the time we got there, just like we thought. Callum was eating a sandwich in the kitchen, and I don't know where Veronica was. Possibly at cheerleading practice or some such thing; she was always involved with things like that.

"Hey, Tyke, you want to play a game?" Callum asked as soon as we walked in. I was the only one he could con into playing against him anymore, so he never missed an opportunity to ask. Well, besides Philip, anyway, but that was different. Callum was the baby of the family and I think that's why Philip had always loved him specially much. Anything he wanted from Philip, he usually got. Most kids would turn into spoiled brats if they got that kind of treatment, but sometimes it has the opposite effect and turns them especially loving and sweet. Or into an atrocious suck-up, if you like to put it that way better. Callum was the sweet-and-lovable suck-up variety.

"Sure, in a minute. Got to wash this salt off, first," I said. Sea salt stings and itches after a while if you don't clean it off, and I was determined to get a shower before I did anything else. Jesse was already using the upstairs one, so I used the shower in Aunt Joan's room. I came out toweling my hair dry, and put on some of the freshly-laundered clothes she'd set on top of my dresser for me to put away. They smelled like mulberries, the scent of the fabric softener she likes to use. Maybe I noticed all those little things because I knew I'd have to give them up so soon; within hours, actually. Loss tends to make even tiny things poignant.

I just hoped we could convince Uncle Philip that this was a serious issue worth risking his life for. The Breyers and the Weisses had been scientists, and with them the data could speak for itself, almost. But Philip Carpenter was a construction contractor, and science was almost like a foreign language as far as he was concerned.

We had our work cut out for us, that was for sure.

Philip surprised me, though. He didn't question the fact that the bacteria might kill everybody on Earth, maybe because by that time we'd started to hear the first trickle of news reports out of India about the horrific numbers of victims. It had already spilled over the border into Bangladesh, too. There wasn't the slightest hint yet about any cases popping up elsewhere in the world, but I knew that was only a matter of time.

"Yeah, I've heard of it. Can't help but see the news," Philip agreed when I asked if he knew anything about the Orion Strain.

"Then you know how deadly it is, right?" I asked, and he nodded.

"Well, I was at school the other day, and I found out it can affect warm-blooded animals, too. Any bird or mammal," I said, and then waited for him to connect the dots.

"But they'd never be able to contain something like that," he objected.

"Exactly," I said, and he shook his head.

"Why haven't they said anything about it, if that's the case?" he asked.

"Would you want to cause a panic over a deadly disease, if there was nothing you could do to stop it?" I asked, and he frowned.

"We think it'll reach the Tampa area within the next few days, but we've got a survival plan," I went on, and then told him about the Moon project.

"Who's this 'we' you keep talking about?" he asked.

"Me and Jesse, Dr. and Mrs. Weiss from school, and Mr. and Mrs. Breyer, Drew's parents. It's a serious thing," I said, hoping and praying he'd believe me.

"We think everybody should come, Dad. You and mom, Chris, Callum, and Veronica," Jesse added.

One of the worst faults of many parents is that they don't take their kids seriously. They always think you're ignorant and that you don't know what you're talking about. But Philip wasn't like that. He was the type of man that if his son told him something, no matter how wild and crazy it seemed, he'd simply believe him no matter what, and then defend him to the bitter end.

Jesse and Chris had earned that kind of trust by never lying to him, and it stood all of us in good stead, now. Oh, they might have fibbed about who ate the last piece of chocolate cake in the refrigerator or some little thing like that, but they'd never lie to him about something like this, not when lives were at stake. They knew it and he knew it, and more than any other reason, I think it's why he believed us that day.

"When did Dr. Weiss think we should leave?" he finally asked, and I knew we'd won.

"Tomorrow morning, while we know we've still got time. Before the plague has a chance to get here," I said.

"I'll need to call a few people before then," Philip said, and I glanced at Jesse.

"Uh. . . Dad, Dr. Weiss really didn't want us to tell anybody except the people who are coming," he said reluctantly. Philip looked stern.

"Dr. Weiss may be a fine man, and I'm grateful to him for offering us a chance like this. But we owe it to those other people to at least let them know, so they can try to make some kind of arrangements for themselves, too. If the shoe was on the other foot, that's how I'd want them to treat us. We owe them that much," he said.

I knew Dr. Weiss wouldn't like that idea, but if he got mad then he'd just have to get mad. Once Philip Carpenter made up his mind about something, you were wasting your breath to try to change it.

"Did you ask about Emily?" Chris asked, speaking for the first time. He'd waited for his father to finish talking out of respect, but naturally he wanted to know about his girlfriend.

"Yeah, she can come if you can talk her into it. So can her parents and her sister. But you've got to convince them before we leave in the morning," Jesse told him. Chris looked at his watch; it was already nearly four o'clock.

"I better go talk to them," he muttered, and excused himself. Philip and Joan spent about thirty minutes on the phone, warning everybody they knew or could think of, and then silence settled over the room. Even Callum and Veronica were quiet.

"It sounds to me like there might be some tough times ahead for a while, so what do you say we go out and do something to take our minds off the whole thing for a while?" Philip finally said.

So that's what we did. We loaded up in the van and went out for mini-golf. Maybe it sounds like a strange way to spend your last night on Earth, but it was fun anyway. The place we went to had a pirate's cove theme and there was a real waterfall and a pirate's ship. Philip put Callum up on his shoulders and carried him around half the night, even though he was really too big for that kind of thing anymore.

Then we went for ice cream before heading home. Dr. Weiss had told us to be at his house in Zephyr Hills no later than eight o'clock in the morning. If we weren't there by then, he'd leave without us.

Somehow I didn't doubt he meant it.

Chapter Four

Chris showed up with Emily and her family not long after we got home, and I was shocked to see Chris wearing a wedding ring on his finger. He hadn't said a word about getting married, and I don't think Aunt Joan and Uncle Philip were all that pleased that he'd done something like that without even telling them, first. From what I gathered later, Emily hadn't told her parents, either.

I guess there must have been some serious discussion for a while, about that and everything else. I don't know what all was said because Philip sent us upstairs, but the upshot of the whole thing was that the four of them agreed to go.

"Do you think this'll really work, Tyke?" Jesse asked in a low voice. We were supposed to be in bed, and I guess he didn't want anybody to hear him.

"I don't know. We'll either make it or we'll die trying," I said, trying to make it sound like a joke. But it came out sounding way more serious than I thought it would.

"Yeah, true. It's weird, Chris getting married, isn't it?" he said, changing the subject.

"Yeah, I never saw that one coming," I admitted. Chris and Emily had been going out for nearly a year, but he'd never breathed a peep about marriage. He was only eighteen, after all. I don't know what on Earth he was thinking, unless maybe they thought it might help convince her parents to come along. But that's only a guess.

Jesse must have been tired, because he didn't say anything else and before long I could hear him snoring.

I knew I ought to get some sleep myself, but I had too many thoughts in my head and I was too keyed up for that. I think it was nearly one o'clock before I finally drifted off.

Aunt Joan woke us up early, buzzing around the house like a bumblebee making sure everything was packed and ready. It gave everything a carnival-like feel, like we were about to leave on a family vacation or a trip to the zoo, instead of getting ready to make a desperate run for our lives.

Most of the neighborhood was still asleep when we stumbled out to the van, still half asleep ourselves. It looked like any other ordinary day, and I guess maybe it was for the time being. But it was the last ordinary day there would ever be.

Philip drove us across the causeway into Clearwater proper, and then across Old Tampa Bay and down by the airport. There were still planes landing and taking off, so they hadn't closed down air travel just yet. Not that it would make much difference even if they did, sadly, but I guess I expected them at least to go down fighting.

"Stupid," I muttered, looking at the jets.

"Yeah, but there's nothing we can do about it except pray for them, Tyke," Jesse said.

It was still too early for the traffic to be bad, so we made it out to Zephyr Hills in less than an hour. There were already three other cars in the Weiss's driveway. One of them belonged to the Breyer family, but I didn't recognize the other two.

"That's Leah's mom's car," Jesse murmured, pointing to one of them.

"What about that one?" I asked, nodding my head at the other car.

"No idea," he said.

Dr. Weiss had rented a charter bus to carry us all to MacDill. I'm sure it must have cost a fortune, but then on the other hand money soon wouldn't mean anything anyway.

We unloaded from the van and boarded the bus in a reasonably orderly way. Besides the Carpenter clan and associates, I spotted the Breyer and Weiss families, and Aron Anderson. I also recognized Amos and Katrina McClendon from the Academy; she was my biochemistry teacher, and I knew he was one of the physics instructors even though I'd only seen him once or twice. They had their little daughter with them, but I couldn't remember what her name was.

The other people I didn't know from Adam. There was a lady and a little boy with Leah, who I assumed were her mother and brother. Aron had his brother and sister and his parents with him; they all looked too much alike to make any mistake about that. The only other person was a tough-looking teenage girl maybe sixteen years old, with a five year old boy in tow. I'd never seen her before in my life, but I guessed she was one of Bethany Weiss's friends since those two seemed to be spending a lot of time together.

That was it. I counted up rapidly and made out thirty-two people.

"We've got too many people," I said, turning worriedly to Jesse.

"Yeah, I noticed that, too. I wonder who the odd man out will be," he said, sounding just a little uneasy. Something hadn't gone according to plan, and whenever that happens then you never know what might have to change. Dr. Weiss might not hesitate to kick somebody off the list if he thought he had to.

It was about a two hour drive down to MacDill; the morning rush hour had started by then and it was all we could do to creep along at thirty miles an hour in places. I put the time to good use, by finding out as much as I could about the people I didn't know very well.

The most interesting one turned out to be the tough-looking girl I'd never seen before; Danielle Black.

From what I heard, she was one of Bethany Weiss's weed dealers and a part-time shoplifter who'd been in and out of juvenile detention since she was twelve. The little boy was her nephew, Derrick.

For a while, I was shocked that Dr. Weiss had ever agreed to let such a person come along at all. But then I heard that Bethany had thrown a huge tantrum and threatened to blow the whole mission unless Danielle and Derrick could come. Bethany must have been good at getting her own way; I've got give her that much. It seemed strange that two mild-mannered scientists could have produced such a strong-willed daughter, but obviously they had.

I also heard that Amos McClendon's mother had refused to come along when he'd asked her; she thought the whole thing was bosh, and nothing he or anybody else said could convince her to change her mind. Amos had decided to go ahead with the plan anyway for his daughter's sake, but he sat in the front row of the bus looking tight-lipped and grim, and it was easy to guess how much it must have broken his heart.

There were other stories like that. Several of the kids at school who'd been asked to go wouldn't believe there was any danger, or else they thought it was safer to hole up somewhere on Earth than to try such a risky plan as ours.

Mrs. Weiss had arranged things at MacDill so they thought she was leading a field trip from the Academy, and Dr. Weiss had told the school the same thing so the story would check out if anybody called. The secret wouldn't keep for long, of course, not with all the people who knew about it, but hopefully it wouldn't have to.

The bus had TV screens in the back of each seat, and Jesse was watching the morning news beside me.

"Uh-oh, here it comes," he said, nudging me in the ribs. They were doing a special report about the Orion Strain; apparently they now had confirmed victims in thirty countries, including three in California. That was way too close for comfort.

People were beginning to wake up to the danger, too; the news anchor kept talking about how this and that were being done, and how they expected a vaccine to be available within a day or two, and how there was no need for alarm, and so forth.

It scared me more than I like to admit. The germ was spreading even faster than I'd feared it would, and it could show up in Tampa at any time, maybe even before we had a chance to leave. I started looking suspiciously at every bird we passed, wondering where it might have come from and whether it was infected or not.

We finally reached the main gate at MacDill, and the bored-looking guard waved us through with no trouble once he saw Mrs. Weiss's security badge.

MacDill Aerospace Research Center covers a lot of territory. It's built on a peninsula that sticks out into Tampa Bay, and it had once been an air force base a long time ago. Now it was a sprawling research park, devoted to aerospace engineering and related pursuits. They had a close working relationship with several universities, companies, and even with the Academy; Tabby and Jesse had taken some of their classes there, now and then.

I don't know exactly what Mrs. Weiss's job was, but she was pretty high on the totem pole out there, at least in the department that was working on the XR-339. It took us about thirty minutes to make it from the front gate to the west airfield, and when we got there she parked the bus beside the hangar.

We all climbed off onto the tarmac, and presently Mrs. Weiss opened the main hangar door and led us inside. There weren't many people around when we went indoors; just a couple of techs doing whatever it is that techs do. They glanced up, saw Mrs. Weiss with a bunch of mostly kids wearing backpacks, and looked away again without batting an eye.

She started telling us about the history of the XR series and how they weren't used much anymore because of costs and technical issues and safety concerns about working with thorium fuel cells because they were so dangerously radioactive, and so forth. By the time she got done, I didn't wonder that nobody wanted to use the XR's anymore. I wouldn't have, either.

Then she gave us a cheery little pep talk about how she believed those problems could be solved and the XR would have a bright future again, just like she was really teaching a group of interested field-trippers. We played along with it, nodding and pretending we were interested. The ship in front of us was named the *Cabral*, she said, after Pedro Cabral, the Portuguese explorer who first discovered Brazil. It was sleek and white, with a bright red stripe down the side. Its sister ship in the hangar next door was the *Balboa*, named for the Spanish explorer who first laid eyes on the Pacific Ocean. She never did say what the reason was for the famous-explorers theme, and I didn't feel inclined to ask.

After she'd talked for about thirty minutes, she finally went up to the airlock door of the *Cabral* and casually opened it, like she meant to give us a tour of the interior. We filed inside one by one, and as soon as we were out of sight of the techs she started telling us to put our bags in the overhead compartments before we found a seat and buckled our belts. The *Cabral* really reminded me almost exactly of a regular plane, except it was smaller, of course, and it had an airlock instead of a normal door.

Besides the pilot and copilot seats where Mrs. Weiss and Mr. Breyer sat, there were twenty-nine more seats, and sure enough, we turned up one seat short. Dr. Weiss turned to Danielle with a scowl.

"Hold him. If he gets hurt then that's just too bad; you shouldn't have brought him," he told her. Danielle didn't say a word, and for once even Mrs. Weiss looked embarrassed. But Danielle quietly buckled Derrick in next to her, sharing a seatbelt even though you're not supposed to do that.

I wondered why we hadn't taken the *Balboa*, also, since there were two planes. It seemed to me like we could have saved twice as many people that way, as long as we had a pilot. I even mentioned the idea to Drew, and the only answer I got was that Dr. Weiss thought it was too risky. I'm not sure exactly what that was supposed to mean, unless it was simply the fact that the more elements you involve in a plan, the more likely it is that something will go wrong.

For a while, Mrs. Weiss and Mr. Breyer were busy doing systems checks and so forth, to make sure everything was in good shape before we tried to leave. We definitely didn't need any mechanical problems.

I looked out the window at the tarmac and the Tampa skyline, and wondered if I'd ever see any of it again. So many things could go wrong before we ever had a chance to come home. So very, very many things.

A few minutes later Mrs. Weiss shut the airlock, buckled herself in, and started the engines. I'm not sure what the techs must have been thinking at that point; maybe they thought she was just doing an elaborate demonstration. But when the wheels started to move and we gradually rolled out of the hangar onto the tarmac, they must have decided enough was enough. I heard somebody radio the cockpit, and even though I couldn't quite make out what they said or what Mrs. Weiss replied, they sure didn't sound very happy. She paid no attention.

By the time we made it out to the runway they were practically screaming at her, loud enough that everybody in the plane could hear. I made out something about us not having clearance for an unauthorized flight and a bunch of cussing and static and then a threat to have Mrs. Weiss fired and jailed as soon as she landed, and who knows what else.

Mrs. Weiss just chuckled and started revving the engines. Then she released the brake and we moved faster and faster until I felt us leave the ground.

She took us out across the Bay and skimmed so low over Saint Petersburg that I could have sworn she was about to knock the tops of the buildings off, but then we were out over the Gulf and steadily climbing higher. She quickly circled around to head east and thereby get a boost from the Earth's rotation, and I'm sure she must have caused migraines to every tower controller in the area, popping completely unannounced into heavy air traffic like she did. It's a wonder we didn't cause a mid-air collision.

Then we were up, and up, and up some more, till the sky started to fade from blue to dusky purple and finally to black. I felt the *Cabral* lurch before it settled down into what felt like stillness, even though I knew we were moving very fast indeed.

"That was a wild ride," I commented.

"Yeah, I think she got her pilot's license out of a gumball machine," Drew said. At first I agreed with him, but after I got to thinking about it I decided maybe what looked like insane flying was really excellent flying. She'd had to deal with crowded skies, a quick departure, and all kinds of things, and yet she'd managed to get us away without crashing the plane or killing us. So maybe she was a better pilot than I thought. Or maybe she was just insane.

After a while, I noticed that gravity was falling in the cabin, and after a little while longer it faded away almost completely. Several people were sick, then, and the vomit bags got put to good use. Zero gravity tends to make people ill, just like motion sickness only worse. The sour, nasty smell of vomit filled the whole plane, and that by itself was enough to make me want to vomit myself. Somehow I managed to keep my breakfast down, but I won't say it was easy.

For the next three days we had to survive like that; zero gravity, buckled into our seats most of the time, most of us nauseated either by the lack of gravity or the stench of old vomit, never able to see anything except the blackness of space. A few people had been smart enough to bring books, and they were the lucky ones. The rest of us just suffered.

It got cold and stayed cold, because Mrs. Weiss didn't dare use any more energy than she had to for heating; she had to save it for propulsion. We put on extra clothes and huddled together for warmth when we could.

She kept the radio turned on and now and then we heard things from Earth, most of it bad; how the Orion Strain was spreading like wildfire, and how many millions of people were dead or dying and what the government was trying to do about it. Sometimes being right is truly awful.

Then the broadcasts faded into prayers, and finally into dead silence even before we reached the Moon. I remember wondering if anybody was still alive down there at all, or if we were really the only human beings left in the universe. It was a lonely thought.

Late on the third day we came in sight of the Moon itself. It was a cloudy day down there, but through a break in the clouds we could see the Stormy Ocean and the Sea of Tranquility, and between them the long peninsula which the survey teams had named Terra Nevaia, the Land of Snow, from all the white stone down there.

The shape of it reminded me of Florida, sort of, if you imagined Florida being upside down and backwards. Just then I heard Mrs. Weiss key the microphone.

"Ladies and gentlemen, we thank you for flying with us. If you'll direct your attention to the tip of the peninsula beneath us, you'll catch of glimpse of Lake Okechobee right there in the middle, and just to the north the Snowy Mountains. Right there on the north shore of the lake is Lakeside Station, our temporary home for the next few years. Temperature at the Station is currently 132 degrees Fahrenheit, with thunderstorms to the west. We'd like to welcome you to the lovely and exotic shores of the Moon, and we hope your stay here is a pleasant one," she said. I was sure I detected irony in her voice, but no one laughed. I smiled at the name of the lake; somebody else must have noticed the resemblance to Florida, too.

Hours passed, and again there was nothing much to do except wait, and talk about what things might be like down on the surface, and so forth. I was sitting next to Drew again at the time, so I had a better source of information than most of the others did.

"What do you think it'll be like down there?" I asked, still peering out the window. The clouds made it hard to see much of the land, and what little I could see wasn't very informative.

"It'll probably still be hot when we get there; I know that much," he said.

"You think so?" I asked.

"Yeah. The sun shines for fourteen days straight, so things get pretty warm. We're starting to slip around toward the night side, now, but I bet it'll still be over a hundred degrees down there when we land," he said.

"Yuck," I murmured.

"I hope we can get the air conditioner up and running pretty soon," he said.

"You think it'll still work after all this time?" I asked.

"No telling, really. They probably built things pretty tough, knowing what kinds of extreme conditions they'd have to go through up here. So hopefully," he said.

"Mmm," I nodded, thinking how awful it would be if we had to live down there with no cooling or heating.

"I'm more worried about the food situation than anything else, though," he said in a low voice, and I turned to look at him.

"I thought you said there was a hydroponics lab," I whispered, alarmed.

"Well, yeah, there *should* be, Tyke, but it'll take a few weeks to get anything like that going. I'm just worried about what to do in the meantime. There ought to be some fish and maybe a few other things, though," he said.

"We better hope so," I said, and then tried to put the thought of starving to death out of my mind. I wished Drew hadn't even mentioned it. There was nothing that could be done about it now, and we'd know soon enough anyway. In the meantime all it did was worry me.

The full version of
Tycho
is available now at your favorite retailer.

Author's Note

Cry for the Moon was an interesting book to write. When I first began working on it, I had no idea how things would turn out. The story ended up being much different than I thought it would be at first, with several twists and turns I never anticipated. Books often grow that way, but not usually to the degree that this one did.

Werewolf stories are a hoary old tradition, and there have been countless numbers of them written. But no topic is ever entirely played out, and there are always opportunities to tell a story from a fresh perspective. I hope this one does.

The title has a double meaning. The first is its connotation of wishing for things that are seemingly impossible, as Zach does, and the second is because the full moon (and the monster curse it represents) is the source of so much sorrow to him. Therefore, Zach cries for the moon in two very different ways.

I like Zach very much, after getting to know him so well. His name means "remembered by God", which seemed very appropriate. The book has a serious side that sometimes contrasts sharply with Zach's silly and whimsical sense of humor. He has to face several issues that wouldn't normally be considered amusing by any stretch of the imagination, but he never loses his ability to laugh or his courage in adversity, even when he's very afraid. We could all take a lesson from him.

At bottom, *Cry for the Moon* is a tale of God's grace to one lost in the dark, even though Zach doesn't quite realize that fact until the end. It's also a tale about the cost of virtue, and how no good thing is ever purchased without a dear price.

William Woodall
December 26, 2008

Discussion Questions

1. Zach has grown up all his life in a family of werewolves, and yet chooses not to accept that kind of life for himself. Have you ever had a serious disagreement with someone important to you? If so, how did that make you feel?

2. Zach says that making choices isn't always easy, even when you know what you want. What do you think he meant by this?

3. In order to escape from the werewolf curse, Zach decides to run away from home and find his uncle Justin in Texas, whom he has never met. Do you think this was a wise plan? What else might Zach have done instead?

4. In Sulphur Springs, Zach is mostly afraid of the people who might feel sorry for him and try to help. What do you think about this? Give examples of how it might be possible to want to help someone and yet end up doing them more harm than good.

5. After hearing Zach's story, Justin agrees to let him stay. What are some of the dangers Justin faced by making this choice? Would you have handled the situation any differently?

6. Zach is forced to give up many things by running away, but he also gained some things. Do you think his choice was worth the price he paid? Why or why not?

7. At one point, Zach says that you should never cry for the moon; that is, you shouldn't wish for things which are impossible. How do you feel about that statement? Do you think it's wise, or do you think it might lead people to give up too easily when things seem difficult?

8. Justin tells Zach that it might help him deal with his feelings if he takes the time to write down his story and work it out on paper. In what ways do you think this might be helpful to

someone who is struggling with a difficult problem or painful memories?

9. Although Eileen's feelings are not discussed very much, how do you think she might have felt about Justin's decision to let Zach move in? What do you think Justin and Eileen might have said to each other about this issue?

10. Zach finds it hard to understand why his family won't even talk to him after he runs away. Why do you think they reacted in that way?

11. Why do you think Justin chose to leave Wolfe City after his grandparents passed away, even though he'd lived there in the same house for his entire life?

12. Several times, Zach has to come up with ways to survive and solve problems while he's on the run. Are there any times when you think he could have made better choices or done things differently? Be as specific as you can.

13. Zach does several odd jobs to help him earn money, including raking leaves and cleaning out garages. What are some other things he might have done to earn money?

14. Several experiences in Sulphur Springs make Zach sad, including visiting Stonewall Street and seeing the Christmas decorations up. Are there any places you've ever visited that made you sad or caused you to have other strong feelings? What were those places and why did they make you feel that way?

15. Zach has a hard time deciding what he really thinks about God near the end of the book, although he doesn't say much about it. What are some of the doubts and thoughts you think he might have had?

Praise for
The Last Werewolf Hunter Series!

"If you are looking for a story about a boy who learns valuable lessons about family, love, friendship and God this is the book for you. I recommend this book to a pre-teen or adult. I truly enjoyed this book."
-Rae, *My Book Addiction Reviews*

This author is an excellent writer who knows how to draw the reader into a story and make them feel it. The writing will resonate long after you lay the book   down,"
-Lynn O'Dell, *Red Adept Reviews*

"I found myself captivated with the story and could not stop reading until I reached the final page. Everything about this story is thought-provoking. Readers of all ages will appreciate this wonderfully told story,"
-Jancy Morgan Dunn, Kansas

"I love this story so much, I'm planning to buy it in its paperback form,"
-April, Southern California

"Unlike any story I've ever read before,"
-Jennifer Slattery, Missouri

The Last Werewolf Hunter: The Complete Series
*is available now in print and ebook editions
at your favorite retailers!*

Book One: Cry for the Moon

Book Two: Behind Blue Eyes

Book Three: More Golden Than Day

Book Four: Truesilver

Tycho
By William Woodall

In the year 2154, sixteen year old Tycho McGrath is an advanced genetics student at the prestigious John Brooke Academy in Tampa. Life seems fairly dull, until he accidentally discovers that in less than a week, a recently designed bacterium known as the Orion Strain will almost certainly wipe out every human being on earth.

Tycho and his friends quickly form a desperate plan to steal an experimental spacecraft and flee to the partially-terraformed Moon, hoping to ride out the plague until it's safe to come home.

But the survivors of Earth soon discover that the Moon has its own dangers. Horrific storms, radiation poisoning, and mutant insects all lie in wait for the unwary, and worst of all, they must soon face the betrayal of one of their own.

This book also features Cameron from *The Last Werewolf Hunter*. Tycho is his nephew.

* * * * * *

"Reminiscent of Freedom's Landing, by Anne McCaffrey, Tycho combines the best of traditional space-exploration sci-fi with modern apocalyptic fiction. For any fans of hard science fiction, it doesn't get any better than this,"
-Liz Ellor, Virginia

"Woodall tells an interesting sci-fi story, through the eyes of Tycho the young scientist,"
-David King, Missouri

Available now from your favorite retailer!

Unclouded Day
By *William Woodall*

Brian Stone's life isn't easy. Abandoned by his father, abused by his alcoholic mother, and mocked by his classmates, his only treasures are his beloved little brother and his old guitar.

Then Brian finds a magical amulet in his attic, and things begin to change. Soon he has more power and wealth than he's ever dreamed of, and for a while all seems to be well.

But Brian has made a terrible mistake which may cost him everything, and his only hope is to seek out the Fountain at the Heart of the World, wherever *that* may be.

Unclouded Day is a tale of the glory of God's love; the life-giving Life, and the Beauty that makes beautiful.

* * * * * * *

"I would absolutely, without reservation, encourage you to read this wonderful novel, even if you aren't the fantasy genre type. It was a blessing."
-Sue Collier-Brannin, Reflections and Reviews

"There are so many nuggets of truth hidden in this book. It's about Heaven. It's about bad things happening for a reason. It's about deciding for yourself what matters most in life. It's a really good book!"
-Tattie Maggard, Christian Fiction Ebooks, Missouri

"William Woodall has the gift of writing , well, what I'd call young adult stories, though anyone could read this and be blessed,"
-Anna Rashbrook, England

Available now from your favorite retailer!

Many Waters
By *William Woodall*

Cody McGrath is a young cowboy with big dreams and some dangerous enemies. Lisa Stone is a small-town waitress with problems of her own. But when a prophetic dream forces them uneasily together, they soon discover that love can blossom even under the most unlikely of circumstances.

Many Waters is a sweet tale of first love, but it's also a story about living for God and not for the world, about courage and faith and greatness of heart even when the odds seem impossible.

In this book you will find Matthieu Doucet from *The Last Werewolf Hunter*, Brandon Stone from *Unclouded Day*, and several other characters. Additionally, Cody and Lisa are Tycho McGrath's grandparents.

* * * * * * *

The Prophet of Rain
By *William Woodall*

It is written, in the Book of the Prophets, that the Most High knows all the desires of our hearts, and that such things are never passed by without answer. When a boy named Jeremy daydreams of adventure and greatness, he never imagines what that wish will get him into.

As he is pulled from boredom to slavery to greatness, into fighting wicked Kings and monsters, living among barbarians who would like nothing better than to kill him, and finally defending his land against the greatest danger it has ever faced, Jeremy discovers that to be called of God is a frightening and dangerous thing, but always worthwhile in the end.

Available now from your favorite retailer!

If you'd like to find out more about these books and others, please visit:

**William Woodall's
Official Author Website**

www.williamwoodall.org

Here you will find:

Free short stories

Discussion questions for teachers and book clubs

Free sample chapters of all my books

Photos of characters and locations for each story

Articles

Interviews

Quotable Quotes

Contact Information

And much, much more!

Printed in Great Britain
by Amazon.co.uk, Ltd.,
Marston Gate.